Miracles and Conundrums
of the Secondary Planets

Miracles and Conundrums
of the Secondary Planets

·········· *Stories* ··········

Jacob M. Appel

Black
Lawrence
Press

Black
Lawrence
Press

www.blacklawrence.com

Executive Editor: Diane Goettel
Cover and book design: Amy Freels

Published 2015 by Black Lawrence Press.
Printed in the United States.

The following stories have previously appeared, sometimes in different form, in the following publications:
"Miracles and Conundrums of the Secondary Planets" in *Gettysburg Review*, "Phoebe with Impending Frost" in *Southwest Review*, "Invasive Species" in *Alaska Quarterly Review*, "The Resurrection Bakeoff" in *Conjunctions*, "The Orchard" in *Phoebe*, "The Grand Concourse" in *Threepenny Review*, "Measures of Sorrow" in *StoryQuarterly*, and "Shell Game with Organs" in *Boston Review*.

For Rosalie

Contents

· · · · · · · · · · · · · ·

Miracles and Conundrums
of the Secondary Planets

· ·

Zigfrīds Imants Lenc did not have a name on his home planet,
because names were superfluous, but in Lummings, Alabama,
where he operated the Latvian restaurant opposite the abortion
clinic, his regulars called him Red Ziggy. The "Red" did not refer
to the young man's politics. Customers at Café Riga found the
eatery's proprietor zealously neutral in political matters, as imper-
vious to provocation as the mimes at the Twelve Oaks Mall. Newcomers often speculated that his colorful nickname arose from
the young man's perpetually blush-slapped cheeks: a plausible, yet
inaccurate guess. Rather, Ziggy had purchased the eatery from
an old-timer known as Red Wally, who'd once made headlines for
refusing Rosa Parks a soft drink. Ziggy replaced his predecessor's
ham hocks and black-eyed peas with pickled mushrooms and black
balzam; the food critic at the *Press Sentinel* plucked the "Red" off
Wally and pinned it onto Zigfrīds. But the review itself had been
generous. Café Riga could claim to be the only Latvian restaurant
in metropolitan Birmingham—the only Latvian restaurant in the
entire state, in fact—which explained Red Ziggy's placement. If
the proprietor knew little about Baltic cuisine, his clientele knew

even less, so mistakes were unlikely to attract attention. This low profile suited his mission: to observe the outlying planet's inhabitants. Unfortunately, Dr. Schnabel opened his clinic six weeks after Red Ziggy baked his first *pīrāgi*, drawing competing demonstrators and the national media to Lummings; four months later, Erin Gwench of Saint Agatha's College in Creve Coeur, Rhode Island, came to torment his soul.

She'd sauntered into the café one summer morning, alone, wearing a striped "CHOOSE LIFE" T-shirt, which accentuated her full chest, and a floral print skirt with a flounced hem. Already, her arrival—at 11:00 am—distinguished her from her fellow protestors. Most of the activists from both opposing camps lunched in packs, like hyenas, using meals to bond and gossip and organize. Red Ziggy seated them in separate sections: pro-lifers beneath the portrait of Prime Minister Kārlis Ulmanis, the Father of Latvian Independence, and pro-choicers by maps of the Livonian seacoast. Occasionally, one of these zealots might direct Ziggy's attention to the opposing enclave—to point out a diner who'd allegedly condoned infanticide in a journal article, or had supposedly done prison time abroad for transporting explosives—but for the most part, once under Café Riga's neutral roof, the two armies ignored each other. During the nine weeks since the demonstrations had started, Erin was the first protester to desert the picket lines for the restaurant on her own schedule, and the only activist to request a table for one.

The girl was sharp-featured and willowy—an anomaly among the corn-fed young women who carried placards depicting bloody fetuses. If not for her T-shirt, Red Ziggy would have assumed her to be a patient escort visiting from Berkeley or NYU. He'd served several of these young women—but fortunately none who studied the culture of Eastern Europe. Although he listened to his audiotapes every evening, struggling to master a Latvian accent, he still sounded more like an intoxicated Swede. Or possibly an American stand-up comedian impersonating an intoxicated Swede.

Red Ziggy provided his own table service before five o'clock.

"You're not waiting for your friends, miss?" he asked.

"I had breakfast with them," she answered. "That was more than enough socializing for one day. Besides, I got hungry, and when my blood sugar dips I'm thoroughly useless."

She scanned the laminated menu and a faint crease appeared above her delicate nose.

"We have a delicious fatty piglet in aspic today," announced Red Ziggy, emphasizing the delicacy's flavor by kissing his fingertips— as he'd seen a Greek chef do in a film. "Or I can start you off with a pork-and-sorrel soup, followed by a salted herring in a rye blanket. How does that sound?"

The girl grimaced. "Very bloody," she said. "Do you have anything vegetarian?"

Vegetarianism was not an issue on Red Ziggy's home planet, where organic molecules were absorbed from the atmosphere through the skin. Nearly every item on Café Riga's menu paid homage to hogs, even the milk-simmered pilchards, into which the proprietor generously stirred shards of bacon. Usually, this suited the diners of Lummings just fine. But the auburn-haired creature gazing up at Ziggy, her eyes both hopeful and exacting, seemed to share as little with the diners of Lummings as he did.

"I can make you a strong borscht," offered Red Ziggy. "I also have a fine selection of cheeses . . . I could serve them in a sandwich, if you'd like . . . Maybe our *Ķimeņu siers*—that's our cumin cheese . . . And how about some fresh sliced *Jāņi*? In my native land, *Jāņi* is known as the summer solstice cheese, because it tastes as rich and ripe as the overhead sun."

"That sounds divine," agreed the girl, returning the menu. "I'm sorry to be difficult, but I don't consume animal flesh because I believe that all life has intrinsic value. Some of those people you called my friends *claim* to be pro-life, but then they barbecue chickens for dinner. So what they really mean is that they're opposed to killing *human* babies, but they don't mind if Frank Perdue breeds crippled birds and tortures them to death."

Ziggy smiled politely. "Would you like a soft drink or an iced tea with your meal?"

"I'm okay with water," answered the girl. "Now can I ask *you* a question?"

"Certainly, you may *ask*," said Red Ziggy—his well-honed response.

He stood with his hands in his apron pockets, prepared to defend his nonalignment. The girl was his only customer. Outside, a protestor barked through a bullhorn.

"Which side are you on?" demanded Erin.

"I'm on neither side," explained Red Ziggy. "I am sworn to neutrality."

This response was usually greeted with an intense attempt at conversion—a long lecture on reproductive freedom or the rights of the unborn. But Erin made no effort to convince him that Dr. Schnabel was a murderous butcher. All she said at first was, "That's too bad," and then she asked if he had any chopped fruit or berries available to accompany her lunch.

When Red Ziggy returned several minutes later to serve the steaming borscht, she was reading a book titled *Middlemarch* by a man named Eliot. She tasted the soup, while he waited with his circular tray under his elbow, and she nodded her approval.

"You'll forgive me for asking this," she said, "but may I inquire *why* you are sworn to neutrality? I could understand if you were on the other side—in that case, you'd be mistaken—deeply misguided, in fact—but at least you'd be morally engaged. But *neutral*? How can you watch what's happening on your own doorstep every day and not care?"

Her expression wasn't angry, but genuinely puzzled. He wondered how she might respond if he told her the truth: That on his home planet, both abortion and childbirth were equally unthinkable. If a couple desired offspring, they merely wished it so—and the infant materialized. Similarly, death occurred when one willed an end to living. These were the fundamental truths of Ziggy's upbringing, but he feared they might not translate: the inhabitants of the minor planets often lacked imagination. In any case, such candor was strictly forbidden.

The girl kept her platinum-flecked eyes locked on his, her manner open and encouraging, like a schoolteacher trying to coax wisdom from a bewildered child. He removed his spectacles and wiped them on his butcher's smock.

"Caring is bad for business," he finally said. "I have no opinion."

"I disagree," objected the girl. "I can see how *sharing* your opinion might be bad for business. But you must have one, don't you?"

Red Ziggy glanced toward the door, hoping another customer might call him away—but it was still too early for the midday crowd from the municipal courthouse.

"I'm Erin Gwench," said Erin, extending her pale arm. "I'm a senior at Saint Agatha's College in Creve Coeur, Rhode Island...And let me guess...Don't tell me. You're from someplace in Scandinavia? Sweden?"

Red Ziggy refused to let her speculation faze him. He took hold of her slender wrist and touched his lips to the back of her tiny hand—a gem of traditional European manners that he'd gleaned from one of his training videos. Erin blushed.

"I'm from Latvia," he said. "On the Baltic."

"So we're both newcomers," she replied. "How delightful." She rummaged through her canvas bag and produced a second book. Lettered along the spine, in a complex brocade of snakes and ivy, was the title, *Life: Miracle and Conundrum*. "Can I loan this to you?" asked the girl. "I know you're committed to neutrality, but you might surprise yourself. There's a compelling chapter on moral indifference."

She slid the book across the battle-scarred tabletop. Red Ziggy eyed it suspiciously, as he might a rodent in his pantry.

"I'll just leave it right there," said Erin. "It won't bite."

That was the last word the girl mentioned on the subject. After that, she returned to her own reading, and didn't speak to him again until she requested a doggy bag.

"I can't actually afford to be down here," Erin explained, grinning. "God may have called upon me, but He didn't give me much of a budget."

· · · · ·

Red Ziggy stashed the book in the cabinet beneath the electric purée sieve, alongside the basting syringes and the spare pepper mills—just in the nick of time too, because a Grandmothers-for-Choice contingent wandered into the café moments after Erin's departure. He had no intention of reading the volume, of course. But that evening, after bolting the doors of the eatery, he scanned the thinning crowd of evening protesters for the girl's auburn hair, and he felt a surge of ineffable delight when he finally caught a glimpse of her on the opposite sidewalk, roosting atop an aluminum lawn chair with her nose buried in a book, while two cassocked monks paraded past her counting rosaries. Then Ziggy looked away quickly. When he spotted the coed again the following morning, calling out to a young couple approaching the clinic, he found himself hoping that she might once again indulge her appetite for borscht. Not that he would actually pursue a friendship with this girl—that was, of course, impossible . . . and anything more intimate than friendship was obviously unspeakable . . . but nothing in his orders prohibited casual conversation between acquaintances. What harm was there in that? Alas, the lunch crowd gave way to the dinner crowd and Erin did not return.

That night, in his railroad apartment above the Filipino laundromat, Red Ziggy had difficulty concentrating on his accent tapes, and an even harder time recording his day's observations in his log. Memories of the pale-skinned girl kept intruding themselves into his consciousness: Did she dislike his cooking? Had his swine-cluttered menu offended her? Red Ziggy understood that he was a fool to let this brief encounter burrow so deeply under his mask of human skin, but the restaurateur was light-years from his home planet, and harrowingly lonely, so he couldn't help himself. The next day, around noon, he stepped outside the café on the pretext of hosing down the pavement, and he saw the girl with several of her fellow protesters, picnicking on the far side of the street. They'd laid out a beach blanket—beyond the police sawhorses, in the shade of a tulip tree—and they were eating bag lunches. If he'd wished to, Red Ziggy could easily have crossed Farragut Boulevard and joined the women, but doing so would have irreparably compromised his carefully guarded neutrality. Instead, he retrieved the girl's book from the cupboard and slipped it into the pouch of his apron. Later, once he'd finished his accent-enhancement exercises for the evening, which focused on replacing his hard *v*'s with more airy *w*'s, he settled into the Barcalounger in his bedroom and devoured the volume from cover to cover. Red Ziggy had strong qualms with the book's arguments, which often defied both logic and experience—although no more so than the numerous other political and theological texts that he'd encountered during his stay on the planet. At the same time, Monsignor Thaddeus Craft's crisp prose proved pleasurable reading, and Ziggy assured himself that studying the volume would improve his insight into human thought.

Red Ziggy saw the girl again the following day—shouting at an ancient Black woman accompanying a teenager to see Dr. Schnabel—but once more Erin did not order lunch at Café Riga. He had a hard time reconciling the contemplative being who'd given him a treatise on ethics and the fire-cheeked tinderbox who greeted an elderly stranger with menacing pleas not to "slaughter" her grandchild. But earthlings were always a challenge to pin down. When the weekend arrived and Erin still hadn't returned, Ziggy seriously considered undermining his mission by bringing her a complimentary salad. Fortunately, his love for his home planet overpowered loneliness. So he gave up. He placed Craft's book in the utility drawer, where he also preserved countless novenas to St. Jude and unwanted NARAL flyers, and he forced the auburn-haired girl from his thoughts. That was on Friday night. On Saturday morning, she strolled into the café as though nothing were out of the ordinary, seated herself beneath the portrait of Dr. Ulmanis, and ordered another cheese sandwich.

She was sporting a leather miniskirt and black eyeliner.

"I wasn't sure I'd see you again," said Red Ziggy.

"Some of the girls from Mississippi are also short on money," answered Erin, "so we've been pooling cash for peanut butter and jelly. But I'm done with that..."

"Did God increase your budget?" asked Red Ziggy.

Erin examined him earnestly, as though deciding whether to take offense. "I really did try to make friends—to keep an open mind," she said. "But apparently, the Operation Rescue ladies don't appreciate the way I dress... So I guess I'm committed to an all-cheese-and-borscht diet from now on...." The girl smiled mischievously. "Besides, I *had* to come back. You still have my book."

Red Ziggy glanced nervously at the trio of pro-choice escorts brunching at the far side of the dining room. He said nothing.

"Did you read it?" asked Erin.

"Maybe."

"Do you want to see what *I'm* reading?" Erin reached into her bag—a bright yellow satchel emblazoned with the claim "I SURVIVED ROE V. WADE"—and withdrew a volume thicker than the Douay Bible that Red Ziggy used for a doorstop in his flat. He assumed this book would be yet another treatise on ethics, but upon closer inspection, its title coursed through his arteries like quicksilver: *Latvia: Centuries of Struggle*. Red Ziggy had read a portion of the same history, when he'd first arrived in Lummings. The prose had been far from crisp, and after about fifteen pages, he'd tossed it into the bin with the dishrags.

"It's from the university bookstore in Birmingham," explained the girl, handing him the hardcover volume. "I have five days to return it and I can still get my money back."

"Is *that* ethical?"

"It is on *my* budget," the girl shot back. "And since when are *you* interested in ethics?"

He wanted to respond that, on his home planet, he had a reputation for the highest integrity, that his ethics embraced a cosmic universality that hers lacked. But all he did was smile sheepishly and ask, "Another side order of berries?"

"Sure. Whatever. I didn't come here to talk about berries," she answered—catching him off-guard. "So what did you think of Father Craft's book?"

How easily he could have denied reading it.

"It contained many paradoxes," he said.

"Life is highly paradoxical," replied the girl—seeming pleased to engage him. She rubbed her chin, as though lost in contemplation, yet Red Ziggy suspected that she was working off a previously rehearsed script. "I'll make you a proposal," she said. "Why don't we meet up sometime and talk about it?...Or better yet, I'll help you with Father Craft's paradoxes and you can teach me some basic Latvian. Deal?"

On his home planet, Red Ziggy had been trained to think linearly. The girl's penchant for bouncing between subjects—for connecting theological paradoxes with Latvian linguistics—undermined his defenses. Maybe that was her strategy. But he knew he couldn't teach her even rudimentary Latvian, because he didn't speak a word of it.

"Latvian is a useless language," said Red Ziggy. "Learn Mandarin."

"Do *you* speak Mandarin?" asked the girl.

Ziggy shook his head.

"If God wanted me to learn Mandarin, He'd have sent me into a Chinese restaurant," observed the girl. "But He sent me here, so presumably He wanted me to learn Latvian. It's a divine plan, and I'm afraid you're an integral part of it." She reached for the history text and they each clasped one end of the book for a fleeting moment—as though exchanging a caress through its pages. "How about tonight?" she asked. "After you close up?"

"Not tonight."

"Tomorrow?"

"Next week," yielded Red Ziggy. "Maybe next week..."

That seemed to satisfy the girl. She tucked the volume into her bag. Red Ziggy was on his way back to the kitchen, intending to duck his head under the cold faucet, when she called after him, "Can I ask you one more question?"

He feared the worst—but he returned to her table.

"You like asking questions," he said.

"Sometimes," she answered.

The girl took a sip of water. She gazed toward the kitchen, where a stuffed marlin presided over the swinging doors.

"Well?" he asked. "What would you like to know?"

"I'm just curious," she replied—apparently nervous. "How old are you?"

That would have been such an easy question for an earthling— the sort that these men in Alabama said you could *hit out of the ballpark*. But Red Ziggy still found human time measurements befuddling, and even in his dealings with the wholesalers, he often mixed up weeks and months and years.

"Three hundred fifty," he said.

"Sorry," Erin apologized. "I guess that is none of my business."

"No, excuse me," replied Red Ziggy—his chest welling with shame. "I translate in my head from the Latvian. I meant to say that I am thirty-five." A smile warmed her face, so he added confidently, "*I am thirty-five months old.*"

"You are charming," replied Erin. "*That's* what you are."

. . . . .

Red Ziggy did not know why he'd been taught only English on the home planet or why he'd initially been trained to speak with a Yankee twang. These were matters for the wisdom of his superiors. What frustrated him was that he had not even been equipped with a Latvian phrasebook or dictionary, so he had to drive to a foreign language bookshop in Atlanta on Saturday morning, before the lunch shift, to equip himself for the girl's lessons. They'd agreed upon a Tuesday night rendezvous at his apartment, a twenty-minute walk from the clinic, because Erin lived in a makeshift dormitory with six Carmelite nuns from Baltimore and a pair of twin sisters from a Baptist College in Savannah. Over the next seventy-two hours, when he wasn't baking *speķa pīrādziņi* or stirring sour cream into *skābputra*, Red Ziggy attempted to master colloquial Latvian—to transform the grammar guide's lengthy warnings regarding the declension of pronouns and the pitfalls of the dative case into a means of intelligible communication. He failed miserably. When Erin arrived for her first lesson—radiant as ten thousand suns, a jasmine blossom tucked into her hair—Red Ziggy recalled precisely one phrase of his mother tongue: *Klaju koku visi vçji loka.* "A lonely tree bends to all winds." He stood at the open door, dumbstruck by Erin's glow. The cold reality sank in that his intentions with this girl—whatever they might be—did not comply with either the letter or the spirit of his mission.

"Aren't you going to invite me in?" she asked. "Or—since you *are* the teacher—maybe you should welcome me in Latvian."

"*Klaju koku visi vçji loka,*" he declared.

The greeting appeared to please her. "What does that mean?" she asked.

"A lonely tree bends to all winds," replied Ziggy, as he led her through the narrow foyer. "It's a traditional Latvian greeting."

Red Ziggy offered her the living room's only chair, which he'd set beside a second-hand bridge table. He perched across from her on a stack of milk crates. The apartment was sparsely furnished with Salvation Army bureaus and knickknacks ordered from the online catalogue of the Latvian National Gallery. A lone African violet ornamented the windowsill, absorbing the final rays of twilight. From the laundromat drifted the invigorating scent of cleanser—a pleasure that Red Ziggy could not adequately capture in his log.

The girl wasted no time in flipping open her introductory Latvian text, which fortunately was identical to Ziggy's. She proceeded to read each sentence aloud, periodically turning to her teacher for guidance. Where did the stress fall on *vecu māju*? What was the difference between the conjunctive and conditional mood? She accepted his answers at face value, such as the assurance that the conjunctive and conditional could be used interchangeably. Earthlings, Red Ziggy had discovered, gave the benefit of the doubt to authority figures. In this regard, he couldn't help recognizing, they resembled the denizens of his home planet.

At the conclusion of chapter seven—"Higher Declension Nouns and Adverbial Clauses"—the girl shut the book decisively.

"I'm all Latvianed out," she announced. "Besides, I have another question for you."

"You always do," replied Ziggy, but this time his tone was playful.

Erin rested her pen on her lips for a moment. "Do you think it's unethical to tell a lie for a good cause?"

This was precisely the dilemma that Red Ziggy had been pondering all evening—whether he might omit any mention of the girl from his official report. "I suppose it depends," he replied cautiously, "on the size of the lie and how good the cause is."

"I was afraid you might say that." She glanced over her shoulder, although they were obviously alone in the apartment, and lowered her voice. "My parents think I'm in England for the summer," she said. "They're apolitical—or so they claim—and they were afraid it might be dangerous for me down here, so I told them I was going to London with my friend Bella. I even wrote out eight postcards in advance for her to mail back to them each week. You don't think that's so terrible, Zigfrīds, do you?"

Red Ziggy retrieved a ginger ale from the mini-fridge, split the contents between two scotch glasses, dropped an ice cube in each, and set one down in front of Erin. She was the first person to address him by his full name since he'd arrived in Lummings. This formality boosted his confidence.

"I am glad you did it," said Red Ziggy. "Otherwise, I wouldn't have met you."

She flashed a broad smile. "That's not what I meant."

"Maybe not," Ziggy replied, "but all language is subject to interpretation."

He raised his drink and they clinked their glasses together.

"So what about you?" she asked. "Any deep, dark secrets?"

"I left all of my secrets back in Latvia."

His words sounded more mysterious than he'd intended. He joggled the cube at the bottom of his glass.

"How long have you been in the United States?" she asked.

Another question about time intervals. "Four thousand years."

She laughed. Ginger ale sprayed out her nostrils. She laughed more. And then suddenly she was serious, her hand clasped over his, her breath lapping gently like waves.

"So honestly. What did you really think of Father Craft's book?" she asked.

"I told you. It was full of paradoxes."

"What do you mean?" she pressed.

Red Ziggy knew that he should say nothing. His *duty* was to say nothing.

"If abortion is murder then mass abortion is mass murder," he explained. "Which makes Dr. Schnabel a mass murderer, and since Craft's theory justifies killing to protect large numbers of human lives—such as during wartime—then it follows logically that a person is not only permitted to murder Dr. Schnabel, but that a person has an ethical obligation to do so. Yet Craft also says that doing so is highly immoral. To me, that's a contradiction."

He expected the girl to defend the theologian's argument with an avalanche of contorted logic. Instead, she shrugged.

"I agree," replied Erin. "That's a contradiction."

"And?"

"And I don't have an answer to it. Not yet. But I know that what Dr. Schnabel is doing is immoral and that killing him is also immoral. It may be illogical, but it's true."

"I like logical purity," observed Red Ziggy. "That's why I'm neutral."

"Lots of things aren't logical," she countered. "*Love* isn't logical."

She gathered her books together. "I do hope you change your mind," she said. "You're really far too sweet to not care about those poor babies."

· · · · ·

The chasm between their worldviews did not keep Erin from dining regularly at Red Ziggy's café, often at a discount rate, nor did it prevent additional Latvian lessons on Tuesday and Thursday evenings. Rumors began to circulate among the anti-abortion protestors that "the philosophy chick" and "Mr. Neutrality" were "an item"—but when one of the twins from Savannah hinted at such an association, Ziggy denied it vehemently. "What is a college girl going to see in a working stiff like me?" he asked. "You girls want men with ideas. The biggest idea I've ever had was adding honey to the prune yogurt." Red Ziggy wiped down the woman's table while he spoke. "We have an expression in Latvia," he added. "A man can excel at love or at business, but not both." The saying was entirely of his own creation—but he took pride in how authentic it sounded. As a foreigner from an obscure nation, he'd discovered, one of the easiest ways to endear yourself to Americans was to lace your speech with cryptic proverbs.

What Red Ziggy might deny to others, he could not as easily deny to himself: Erin did prove an endless source of enchantment. She introduced him to the essays of a writer named Kierkegaard,

and taught him how to roast marshmallows, and playfully challenged him to disprove the possibility of miracles. One afternoon
she even skipped out on the protests and convinced him to shutter
the café early—and the two of them drove into the countryside to
see replicas of the European capitals that a Benedictine monk had
fashioned from an assortment of masonry supplies and toilet bowl
floats and cold cream jars.

At first, Red Ziggy had resisted the girl's invitation, fearful that
he might find himself face-to-face with a miniature mock-up of his
"native" city. Thankfully, Brother Joseph's artistry didn't advance
farther east than Warsaw. Once Ziggy made this discovery, he
allowed Erin to lead him from Paris to Vienna to Jerusalem, arm
in arm, like a married couple. While they strolled, she shared anecdotes about Joan of Arc and vividly described the martyrdom of
Saint Cecilia of Sicily. Never had Red Ziggy found his existence
so pleasurable, either on his home planet or on Earth. But he also
knew that he had to break things off—sooner rather than later—
because otherwise, he might actually be tempted to kiss this
auburn-haired beauty. Kissing earthlings was, of course, a gross
violation of his home planet's moral code, *and his own*, particularly
when one had been entrusted with a mission such as his.

He drew lines for himself in the dust: *I'll end this at lunchtime
tomorrow; I'll speak to her after our next lesson.* Yet somehow, listening to her ranting about the immorality of flyswatters, or giggling
at his reference to "Mr. Eliot's" novel, which he'd borrowed from
her, Ziggy always found an excuse for postponing their inevitable
rift by yet another day. But then July drifted in early August, and
the hour approached when he would be required to submit his
seasonal report to his superiors. So what choice did he have? He
decided that he would cut short their friendship at the conclusion
of a long-anticipated trip to the Birmingham Zoo—on the one

Thursday each month that the attraction remained open late into the evening.

Wandering among the exotic mammals of Africa and Australia afforded Red Ziggy perspective. It reminded him that he was as different from this lovely girl as were the echidnas of New Guinea or the tawny ocelots of French Guyana.

They stopped for cotton candy at the concession stand catty-corner to the flamingo marsh and then settled down at a picnic table. Erin picked up the same thread of conversation that she'd momentarily left off while they waited in line.

"I can't help thinking that if I could just convince Dr. Schnabel to read Father Craft's book," she continued—her cheeks as red as her dessert, "he might be persuaded..."

Red Ziggy watched her mouth as she condemned the physician's bodyguards and unveiled her scheme to sneak the book into Schnabel's dry-cleaning. He savored the contrast between her crimson lips and her pale skin. Instead of speaking to her, as he'd intended, Ziggy found himself leaning toward her—magnetized by an irresistible force. On the home planet, of course, one kissed without touching. This was his first human kiss.

She pulled back abruptly. "I can't," she said.

"I don't understand," stammered Red Ziggy. "Did I do it wrong?"

Two pregnant women ambled by, pushing identical strollers. A warm breeze ruffled the dogwoods.

"You did everything just right," Erin answered. "It's only that...I can't let myself feel that way about a man who doesn't share my feelings about other things..."

"By other things," he said sharply, "you mean abortion."

"Yes, about when life begins. But not *only* that," she explained. "At St. Agatha's, I dated a boy from Providence College who ate fish...He was a great guy—charming, intelligent, highly moral

in most regards—eating fish was really the only thing wrong with
him—but he'd take me out to dinner, and I'd see the dead trout or
mackerel with its angry eyeball glaring up at me from the plate,
and eventually I grew to hate him . . ."

And then the girl was sobbing softly, a muted yet intense suffer-
ing. Red Ziggy reached over to comfort her, but she shook away
his embrace. On the wordless hike back to his car, past the silent
giraffes and the raucous marmosets, he felt a haunting distance
between himself and the fauna of this strange planet—as though
even the simplest of earthly life forms might contain mysteries
grand enough to defy an eternity of painstaking observation.

. . . . .

Seven days passed. Each morning, Ziggy watched through the
Persian blinds of the café as the demonstrators assembled—and
each morning, this brief glimpse of the auburn-haired girl imbued
him with enough hope to launch his workday. Much as he'd previously assured himself that their friendship would end at a particular
moment, now he promised himself each morning that this day was
the day that she'd return for a cup of borscht. But she did not. By the
end of that first week without her, Ziggy found himself unable to
focus on his pronunciation exercises. He'd also made no progress with
his seasonal report, which was due at the end of the month. Even his
labors at the restaurant slacked off: Tuesday's grilled boar's snout with
zirnu pikas became Wednesday's pork-and-pea sandwich and later
Thursday's mixed goulash. And then, as if to disprove Ziggy's doubts
about miracles, Friday arrived, and during the height of the lunch
shift, Dr. Schnabel himself appeared at the entrance to Café Riga.

Schnabel was a fierce barrel of humanity, a former paratrooper
descended from South Carolina aristocrats, and his bulletproof
vest swelled the bulk of his jacket. A pair of bodyguards, one burly,

one squat, shielded his perimeter. In the flood of silence that swept across the eatery upon his arrival, enveloping both the physician's supporters and opponents, Schnabel's distinctive drawl requested a table for three.

Red Ziggy's eyes darted from the trio across the dining room and back. The tables beneath the maps of Livonia were all occupied—not by activists, but by a bus tour of Korean senior citizens en route from Graceland to Disneyworld. Ziggy didn't dare seat Schnabel anywhere near the pro-life crowd. So he froze. Sweat beaded his upper lip.

"Is there a problem?" asked Dr. Schabel. "You are serving lunch, aren't you?"

"Certainly," agreed Ziggy, snapping from his inertia. "Right this way."

He led the physician and his entourage to a round table beside the bar, as far from his opponents as possible. Several of these diners turned their back on him. But despite Red Ziggy's apprehensions, no confrontation erupted. Quite the opposite: the nuns and college students seemed cowed by their adversary's presence—as though by ordering a meal, he transformed himself from an iconic enemy into a mere mortal.

Schnabel ordered a stack of meat patties and a bowl of *zidenis*, a porridge traditionally made with pearl barley and beaver tail, but in which Red Ziggy substituted an ear of pig. The bodyguards split a whole roast duck and sampled Latvian beers: *Kimmels* for burly, *Cesu Alus* for squat. They had nearly pared the last gristle from the bird—and Ziggy's blood pressure was slowly settling to its baseline—when Erin returned to the café. She'd trimmed her hair into bangs, and carried her trademark yellow satchel.

Ziggy stepped forward to greet her. The girl nodded at him, but circled around the menu-and-reservation stand and headed directly to Schnabel's table. Both bodyguards were on their feet by the time she'd reached him. One had a hand at his holster. Red Ziggy watched helplessly from a safe distance.

"I want you to read this, doctor," the girl declared—placing Monsignor Craft's book beside the physician's meal.

"No, thank you," replied Dr. Schnabel.

Erin pushed the volume closer to his plate. "If you'll just take a look at it with an open mind," she pleaded, "you might surprise yourself."

The doctor set down his soupspoon and dabbed his chin with his napkin. "Which part of 'no, thank you' don't you understand?" he asked.

"I'll leave it right here," said Erin. "It won't bite you."

"I'm eating my lunch, lady," snapped Schnabel. "Now kindly fuck off."

As he said the words, he swept the book off the tabletop with his elbow. It hit the leg of a nearby chair and landed harmlessly at the base of a plastic fern. The guards advanced toward Erin, but their employer waved them off.

"I've lost my appetite," he said. "Let's get out of here."

Schnabel slapped a hundred dollar bill on the table, where the theology text had been, and walked briskly off the premises. Erin retrieved the book from the floor, dusting the jacket on her sundress. She was still on her knees, holding her hands over her face, when Red Ziggy bent down beside her. He realized that the lunch crowd was watching him, but showing kindness to a sobbing young woman wasn't exactly a breach of his neutrality.

"I'm sorry," he said.

"What are *you* sorry for? He paid for his lunch, didn't he?"

"That's not fair," said Red Ziggy.

He reached for her hand, but she stood up.

"Why isn't it fair?" she demanded. "Sometimes sorry isn't good enough, Zigfrīds. Sometimes neutral isn't neutral at all."

Red Ziggy wasn't sure what made him act—maybe the anguish in her voice, or the emphasis she placed on his Latvian name, or maybe just the sense that he'd never have another opportunity. Whatever it was that moved him—and he had eventually spent several thousand pages of his seasonal report futilely trying to explain his conduct—Erin's words were hardly out of her mouth when Ziggy stripped off his apron and took hold of the book. Seconds later, he was charging through bright sunlight toward the retreating physician.

"Dr. Schnabel!" he called out.

The bodyguards spun around instantly. Their boss turned more slowly. Red Ziggy continued advancing until they stood face-to-face.

"Yes?" asked Schnabel. "We left enough, didn't we?"

"I'm afraid you left more than enough," replied Red Ziggy, pressing the theology book into the doctor's surprised hands. "I don't allow anyone to leave political literature in my restaurant under any circumstances," he said.

"It's not mine," declared Schnabel.

"It is now," replied Red Ziggy. "And as far as I'm concerned, you owe that girl an apology for speaking to her like that. The least you can do is keep her book."

The physician examined the volume, puzzled. Then he tucked it under his arm with a shrug and departed toward the clinic. He was unlikely to read it, Red Ziggy knew—but hadn't he himself also taken the girl's book without ever expecting to open it?

As Red Ziggy walked back toward the restaurant, he realized that the anti-abortion demonstrators were clapping for him. Several hailed his deed with vocal prayers.

Then Erin approached him across the pavement, running, and wrapped her arms around his shoulders. She pressed her magical lips to his. Red Ziggy watched their kiss mirrored in the plate glass window of the café. He had no language to express the wonder he experienced during those precious moments. To anyone else watching the reflection, of course, the two of them looked like ordinary human beings in love.

Phoebe with Impending Frost

. . . .

Likely she's distracted by the snow flurries in May—the last frost usually nips mid-April in this part of Virginia—because she looks at me as though I'm made of uranium. Or maybe it's that I've climbed into the playground through my office window, afraid to lose sight of Phoebe Marboe for however long it might take to exit Whitlock Hall by the main doors. In any case, when I've finally squeezed between the splintered casings and the steel sash, I'm gasping for oxygen and I've managed to shred the sleeve of my cardigan. A sign behind Phoebe, plastered to the wrought iron perimeter fence, warns: *Adults may not enter unless accompanied by a child.* I do not have a child—not with me, nor anywhere else—and I sense the other adults clustered around the sandbox eyeing me warily.

"I saw you through the window," I explain. "I was sitting at my desk and I looked up . . . and *there you were . . .*" And there she *still* is—I can hardly believe it—snow crystals glimmering in her long auburn hair. "Good God, Phoebe. You're as stunning as ever."

"You'll have to forgive me," she answers. "I know this sounds terrible, but I'm afraid I don't know who you are."

"Billy Deutsch. *William*, now," I say, refusing to be discouraged. "You wouldn't date me in high school. Remember?"

She nods noncommittally, hugging her purse to her chest. "Oh, Billy," she says. "Well."

An unruly wind pirouettes through the flurries, churning up eddies of frosted confetti. Overhead, downy clouds play cat-and-mouse with the sun. The women around us—a melting pot of stylish young faculty wives and middle-aged nannies—begin to collect their charges, calling out names and coaxing little arms into windbreakers. From atop the jungle gym, a pudgy boy in fluorescent green knee-shorts hollers that he wants to build a snowman. I know I have only a few more seconds to enchant—or, at least, to disarm—Phoebe Marboe.

"I *teach* here now. At the university," I say. "Whoever would have thought it?"

Phoebe is already looking beyond me, scanning the waves of scurrying children.

"Do you want to have lunch?" I ask. "For old time's sake. We'll celebrate the snow and I promise not to mention a word about how you shattered my seventeen-year-old heart."

She smiles politely and answers, "I'm married." As though this claim requires supporting evidence, she holds up her left hand and displays the ring.

"Happily?" I persist, trying to sound nonchalant.

"Yes, *happily*," replies Phoebe, but she grins, seemingly more entertained than annoyed. "My husband is the new chairman of the folklore department."

"I didn't even know we *had* a folklore department," I say. "You learn something new every day."

That's when the two children descend upon us like bloodhounds. The girl is wearing a fuzzy, one-piece zip-up with a crimson monster's face for a hood. The boy sports a white bucket hat and carries a plastic spider more than half his size. The pair are arguing about whether the snow showers will confuse Santa Claus—with the boy, Oliver, insisting that their Christmas presents might arrive early. When he sees me, he furrows his tiny brow. "Who's *he?*"

"He's an old friend of Mommy's."

"What's his *name?*"

Phoebe looks to me for help.

"William," I say. "My name is William. Like the Conqueror." I wink mischievously at Phoebe and lie without shame: "Your mother went to the high school prom with me."

"*Really*, William," says Phoebe, laughing. "Too much already."

"May I walk you home?" I ask.

"What's a prom?" demands Oliver.

"A prom is a party where high school students go to dance," explains Phoebe as she buttons up the boy's jacket. "And we live right across the street, William, so you'll have to do your conquering elsewhere."

We're the only people still remaining inside the playground. The snow has let up, leaving behind a hoary varnish.

"So much for global warming," says Phoebe.

"Actually," I answer, "it's planetary *cooling* that we should be worrying about."

She flashes me a look of amused doubt. "Is that so?"

"Trust me," I assure her. "I'm a climatologist."

$$\cdots\cdots$$

A fast-moving warm front glides through the next morning, driving the mercury into the low sixties, but then the jet stream shifts and a bitter chill sets in. Records fall up and down the Atlantic seaboard: 34° in Savannah, 28° in Charleston, 19° at Cape Lookout, North Carolina. Here in Laurendale, the cloud cover over the valley traps heat, so we hover around the freezing mark for much of the afternoon. The lead story on the television news is agricultural devastation—how frost damage has wiped out orchards and truck crops from Georgia to New Jersey. Growers predict their peanut yield will be down 95%, worse in some coastal counties; wholesalers estimate that the cost of a bushel of peaches will triple by early June. I'll confess that I derive some unhealthy pleasure from this calamity, as it dovetails neatly with my computer models. I've been warning for more than a decade that greenhouse gases are no match for the aerosol pollutants elevating the planet's albedo and the Milankovitch cycles that have been incrementally tilting Earth's orbit toward an ice age. With these forces already at play, all that's required is a modest decline in solar thermo-magnetic activity—what laypeople call a sunspot minimum—to wreak havoc on farmers across the Piedmont. When I return to my office after teaching my graduate seminar on tornado formation, I'm not surprised to find phone messages from reporters in Richmond and Norfolk.

I spend the next few hours fielding questions on the local radio circuit, serving up my contrarian wisdom in simple and folksy portions. You don't convince anyone of anything by droning on about Spörer's law and Hapke parameters. The interviewers, although skeptical, are far less hostile than usual—and none of the alarmed callers mentions Holocaust denial or the Flat Earth Movement—but as I'm laying out a worst-case scenario for WYNZ's listening audience, forecasting a perpetual daytime twilight and glaciers as far south as the Gulf of Mexico, Phoebe emerges onto the porch of the gabled Victorian opposite the playground. "I have to go," I announce abruptly. "Stay warm." Then I hang up the receiver, scramble through the window and dart across Chickahominy Boulevard.

Phoebe is already inching her hatchback out of the driveway. She appears perplexed when I tap on the passenger window, but she shifts into park and lowers the glass. Her cheeks are flushed from the cold.

"No kids today?" I ask.

"They're with Millard's mother."

"Millard?" I echo.

Phoebe Marboe is married to a folklorist named *Millard*! If I were a schoolyard bully, I could have a field day—but as an allegedly mature adult, I know to hold my tongue.

"Do you want something?" asks Phoebe.

"I thought you might enjoy some company," I answer. "I'm a very good passenger. I can change a flat tire and I pump gas like a pro."

Phoebe rests her forehead on her palm for a moment. "You really are relentless."

"And *you're* married."

"Happily," she answers—maybe flirtatious, possibly just amused.

"I won't forget that."

She throws me a sharp look. *"Don't."*

Her eyes freeze onto mine for what seems like an eternal winter, and then the power locks pop open suddenly. I'm inside the vehicle with my seatbelt buckled before she has an opportunity to reconsider. The carpet beneath the glove compartment is crowded with the relics of middleclass toddlerhood: talking picture books, and stuffed penguins, and a pair of petite, heart-speckled rubber boots. Phoebe twists the heat on to full blast.

We turn down Randolph Street and merge onto the Winchester Pike. Arctic gusts whip the branches of the honey locusts and rattle the road signs. I wait for Phoebe to speak, but she maintains a pensive silence. The cemetery where my mother is buried drifts past on the right. Another ten minutes and we'll reach our old high school in Garnett County, which now houses a satellite of the local vocational college.

"Where are we headed?" I finally ask.

"Shopping," says Phoebe. "They've outgrown their winter clothes." She adjusts the heat to moderate blast and asks, "Were you serious the other day about global cooling?"

"Absolutely. It's not a joking matter," I answer. "But you should probably take anything I say with a few grains of salt."

"Why? Because you're a crackpot?"

"Let's just say the scientific consensus isn't on my side. *Yet.*"

"That's fair enough," agrees Phoebe. "And did I really *shatter* your heart?"

"You don't know the half of it," I say, forcing a cheerless smile.

And she *doesn't* know the half of it. I remember returning to school in first grade—after my mother's final bout with leukemia—and being hugged in the corridor by an unfamiliar, chestnut-maned kindergartener who'd heard about my loss from our art teacher. A decade later, when her own father shot himself to death in the parking lot of the Dairy Queen, I'd already been daydreaming about her for years. By then, of course, Phoebe was hugging boys far more handsome and athletic than I could ever hope to be—but I would pass her at a crowded table in the cafeteria, or spot her wandering alone alongside the drainage ditch beyond the football field, and she always looked so wistful, as though she desperately wanted something other than what she had. When I finally offered something myself—namely *me*, in a handwritten letter taped to her locker door—she responded with a sweet but unambiguous note of rejection. Nineteen years later, I can all too easily rekindle the drowning gloom I experienced as I read her fatal words.

"Maybe *shattered* is a bit strong," I concede strategically. "But I liked you an awful lot. I even drove back down from M.I.T one weekend to see you play Emily Webb in your senior class production of *Our Town*."

"Goodness. Did you really?" she muses. "*That* must have been a disappointment."

"It was the highlight of my freshman year. Pathetic but true," I answer earnestly. "I would have given a kidney to go shopping with Phoebe Marboe back then."

"Phoebe *Alexander* now," she corrects me. "I'm married, remember."

Phoebe switches lanes and pulls into the parking garage of the Sycamore Grove Mall. I follow her across the crowded lot into the Children's Depot and then up the escalator toward the section that stocks winter wear. From the descending stairs of the parallel escalator, a plump, middle-aged matron calls to us, "You're too late," but I don't understand what she means until I see first-hand the depleted racks of jackets and long slacks. I have only witnessed bare shelves like this once before, when I was researching hurricanes in Cuba during the Special Period.

A teenage salesgirl approaches us, smiling apologetically above her navy blue smock. "We're having a two-for-one sale on swimsuits," she says. "First floor, aisle seven." But the girl's pitch is without spirit—as though she knows she might as well be selling magic beans.

"My Papa used to warn us, 'Don't die on one doctor's opinion,'" says Phoebe. "I suppose the same is true with clothing retailers."

Unfortunately, the pickings aren't much better at Creighton's or Kids 'n Things. We do manage to pick up a pair of mittens for Meghan at a boutique in Cloverville and an overpriced hooded sweatshirt for Oliver at the university's bookshop. For my part, I'm not particularly disappointed that there has been a run on warm clothes—that Phoebe will have to phone her divorced cousin in Baltimore for hand-me-downs. I enjoy the feeling of shopping at her side—the familial intimacy of navigating our empty cart through the aisles.

It's nearly five o'clock when we give up our efforts. The air on the arts & sciences quadrangle is crisp with the scent of impending snow.

"So if you're right about global cooling," asks Phoebe, "how cold will it get?"

"I don't know," I answer honestly. "We're talking about a ten to twelve degree drop in the short term—and then the models become erratic."

"So basically, we're screwed."

Phoebe looks so vulnerable in the late afternoon shadows. Her gentle breaths are visible on the frigid air. I wish I could offer her some reassurance, but I can sense that even a comforting hug is now off-limits.

"I'm not a crystal ball," I answer. "But yeah. You could say that."

· · · · ·

The President appears on television that evening, delivering the first of his Oval Office addresses about the cooling crisis. He assures us that the planet is actually growing warmer, that the precipitous bottoming out of global temperatures—which he refers to as a *cold snap*—reflects nothing more than natural variation. His speech is peppered with quotations from the National Academy of Science and the Intergovernmental Panel on Climate Change. What strikes me most is not the content of his address—a haphazard amalgam of hubris and denial to rival Custer on the eve of Little Bighorn—but the pallor in his lips and the noticeable shiver that he displays when he asks God to bless America. The poor fool looks as though he's freezing! At the conclusion of his remarks, the network cameras cut to downtown Washington, where amateur figure skaters are performing toe jumps and Lutzes on the frost-sheathed Potomac. For the briefest moment, one can dream that thermal collapse will lead to a winter wonderland of year-round skiing and backyard Ice Capades, much as the passengers on the doomed Titanic, closing their eyes, could listen to Wallace Hartley's orchestra jazzing up "Songe d'Automne" and pretend that they were reveling in a fashionable Parisian nightclub. This delusion does not last.

It's on the drive to campus the following morning that I first hear about the impending shortages of heating oil and natural gas. Energy providers, anticipating a balmy summer as far north as Canada's Hudson Bay, had cut back drastically on inventories—and we now face a two-to-four-week imbalance before shipments will catch up with demand. I'd made a point of shutting off my cell phone the night before—the only person whom I'd like to hear from is Phoebe, but I realize that's unrealistic—and when I switch the device on again, after savoring two cups of the hottest coffee that Ida's Donuts can muster, the ringing is nearly instantaneous. By the time I've reached the university twenty minutes later, I've been asked on national television whether I believe that the recent cold weather is tied to a rise in the incidence of crop circles or might be the product of fires intentionally lit at Iranian oil wells. Another gaggle of reporters—maybe two dozen, swathed in fleece—shouts questions as I approach my office: Will this deep freeze spell the end of humanity? Do I expect to win the Nobel Prize? Is there anything that *ordinary* people can do to help end the crisis? The journalists pursue me up the stairs of Whitlock Hall as though I'm an indicted felon entering a courthouse. Here is the moment I've long been waiting for: my fifteen minutes of glory. I pause on the neoclassical portico—under the same colonnade where Jefferson once spoke—and I offer my counsel. "Please tell the *ordinary* people, whoever *they* might be, to use their time wisely," I say. "Human beings always find a way to generate heat, but time . . . *time* is perpetually in short supply." I'm very pleased with what I've said, even more so when I hear myself on the midday news. I also enjoy the momentary surge of Elvis-like importance that I experience as one of the campus security guards, sporting an orange knit scarf and matching wool hat, prevents the press from following me into the building.

Pinckney Auditorium is packed for my eight-thirty lecture, swelling with undergraduates whose faces are conspicuously unfamiliar. I'm usually delighted if I hit 50% attendance for an early morning course on cloud dynamics—a requirement for geology majors— but now students have brought along roommates, siblings, dates. How these newcomers expect to benefit from hearing me speak about this abstruse subject without any context or background, I cannot possibly imagine, but I should be thrilled to be the focus of such attention. Had this happened last year, or even last week, I'd have relished holding court at my podium until the next professor arrived to depose me—even if this meant answering questions well into the night. But now, what I want most is to return to my office, to sit at the window from which I can watch Phoebe's veranda. I have thought of her sporadically, at most, for nearly two decades, but since discovering that she lives only shouting distance away—so close that I could cross the avenue and ring her front doorbell, if I dared—my feelings for her have taken on a burning urgency.

I wait at my desk until the last rays of pink sunlight vanish behind the mansard roof of the Episcopal chapel. It is nearly nine o'clock: even though the mercury is plummeting, the days are still growing longer. During the late afternoon, a svelte woman sporting a gypsy kerchief and oversized sunglasses—presumably Millard's mother—arrives at the house with the children in tow and admits them with her own key, before returning to her frigate of a Cadillac and vanishing up Patrick Henry Street. Several hours later, the emperor of the establishment himself appears, on foot, wearing a Stetson fedora and carrying an attaché case. He is handsome—I'll grant him *that*—but his pencil-thin mustache and stubby goatee loan him an aura of affectation, as though he wishes the world to believe him a matinee idol trapped in a folklorist's body. He wipes his loafers on the doormat before entering his castle. Phoebe's hatchback remains parked atop the cusp of the drive. My teenage crush doesn't leave the house. When I finally pull out of the faculty parking lot, the gabled Victorian is shrouded in silhouettes and stands as still as the frozen tombs of Siberia. The thermometer taped to my dashboard reads 14°.

At the age of seventeen, I had a fantasy that the world would come to an abrupt and dramatic end—nuclear winter, germ warfare, collision with a comet—and that, through some generous twist of science, Phoebe Marboe and I would be the only two survivors. To us would fall the responsibility of jump-starting human civilization afresh. I vividly imagined the hours I might pass consoling Phoebe over the loss of her family, tête-à-têtes that invariably concluded with frenzied bouts of passionate lovemaking. That was before I had stumbled through romances of my own—before I'd lived with three successive women, a trio distinguished as much by their complexity as any seductive charms. So maybe the great irony right now is that I don't want to share an ice-locked and lifeless planet with Phoebe. What I desire is to live alongside her *within* a larger community, to savor the warmth of her company among friends and neighbors, to take her waltzing at the Chancellor's ball on graduation night. Like everything else, it seems, the end of the world may arrive too little and too late.

I pull up in front of my own house—and, on impulse, I keep on driving. I recognize that the healthy thing to do at the moment is to rustle up some dinner and to watch the evening news in my pajamas, but a magnetic need draws me back toward Chickahominy Boulevard. I doubt I can ever long for *any* woman today with the intensity that I felt for Phoebe Marboe at the age of seventeen—but if there is one woman I *might* still be capable of feeling that way about, that woman is Phoebe herself, so I park several doors down from her house, trying to appear as inconspicuous as possible. I'm an old hand at idling in front of Phoebe's home. I squandered many nights opposite her front door in high school, waiting for a sign, although *that* house was a *different* house, on a different street in a different town, and, for all practical purposes, Phoebe was a different person. How different *I* am from that lonely, love-struck seventeen-year-old boy is not as clear. What I do remember is that the darkness felt as cold and bitter on those chilling winter nights as it does this evening.

So I wait and, shortly after midnight, I receive my reward. The curtains of an upstairs window are drawn back for a flicker of an instant and Phoebe's regal profile is clearly visible in the moonlight. When I was a teenager, I believed I'd recognized in that face the solitude of a princess imprisoned in a tower, but now all that I see is a mellow warmth—the sort of glowing but steady vitality that might power a human heart for decades.

· · · · ·

The blizzard—which we will later think of as the *first* of the great blizzards—begins insidiously during the night, dusting rooftops and unpaved surfaces. Whirlpools of fine snow spin like white dervishes along the asphalt. By lunchtime, a manna of large, wet flakes has buried the hedges and weighed the magnolia branches to the snapping point. I've given up all hope of encountering Phoebe, and I am making an effort to concentrate on recalibrating my computer models, when the Alexanders' automatic garage door rises like a proscenium curtain and a petite bundle of shag and faux fur steps into the squall. Phoebe carries an aluminum snow shovel with a crimson handle—at first glance, from a distance, it appears as though her wrists are gushing blood. I resist the urge to brave the drifts beneath my office window. Instead, I take a moment to admire my neighbor at her labor. The girl I once worshipped is still a delicate, almost ethereal creature, and she scoops up the snow in birdlike nips. (I'm reminded of a particular anthropology professor-turned-outfielder in our faculty softball league who waits for the ball to stop rolling and then picks it up like a sparrow's egg between her immaculately polished fingernails.) At the rate Phoebe is shoveling, she'll be shoulder-deep in flakes before the storm passes. That's my excuse, at least, for offering to help her, even though it's broad daylight and—for all I know—Millard Alexander is admiring her from his own window. I do make a few concessions to societal norms: I retrieve my winter coat, lock my office door and exit Whitlock Hall by the main entrance, watching my steps to avoid the snow-veiled patches of ice.

When Phoebe sees me approaching, she jabs the shovel into a nearby snow bank and rests her bodyweight on the handle. She appears visibly winded. An arc of perspiration plasters her bangs to her forehead.

"Do you have a second shovel?" I ask.

"Here," she offers. "Take this one. I need a break."

I pick up where she has left off, gripping the tool in both hands, lowering my center-of-gravity as though feeding coal into a furnace. The snow is saturated and heavy as mortar.

"Most people wait to dig out until *after* the snow lets up," I observe. "You can save yourself a lot of extra work that way."

"I guess I'm not *most people*," answers Phoebe. Her tone is defensive, almost snippy—not the sort of response that a man expects when he's clearing a neighbor's driveway for free.

I stop shoveling and turn toward her. "Did I say something wrong?"

Phoebe bites her lower lip. "Promise you won't laugh at me."

"I couldn't even if I wanted to," I answer, heaving a chunk of ice-lacquered snow into the hedges. "I think my laughing muscles are frozen solid."

My companion pulls off a glove, exposing her fine pink hand. She watches pensively for a moment as flakes melt against her bare flesh. I am about to say something else—for the sake of breaking the silence—when she finally speaks.

"I *always* keep my car shoveled out *during* a storm in case there's an emergency," Phoebe explains. "What if Meghan has a seizure like my cousin's daughter? Or if Oliver swallows another nickel?" She conceals her face in her palms for a moment, rubbing her temples, and then glances up nervously. "You don't think I'm crazy, do you?"

"Not at all."

"*Millard* thinks I'm out of my mind."

To hell with Millard, I want to say. Instead, I channel my frustrations against the man's house, running the shovel blade along the cascading ice below his drainpipes, generating a high-pitched symphony as I decapitate stalactites, stratum by stratum, all the way up to the eaves. While I am bolder than I was in high school—I suppose that's what happens when you stop stuttering and earn a doctoral degree—I have also grown far more prudent. So instead of yielding to my reclaimed teenage exuberance and urging

Phoebe to throw her husband to the polar bears, I am determined to broach their marriage far more cautiously.

"You're not saying anything," says Phoebe. "You must think I'm ridiculous."

"Not at all," I reply. "I was just wondering... Honestly, I was wondering whether your husband knows that we're spending all of this time together."

Phoebe shakes her head. "I haven't felt the need to mention it. We don't have that kind of relationship."

I make an effort to sound supportive. "Is it *that* bad?"

"That's not what I meant," answers Phoebe quickly, clearly flustered. "What I meant was that Millard and I trust each other... *implicitly*... We don't tell each other everything because we don't need to."

"I wasn't trying to—"

"It's okay," she replies. "Really."

My instincts tell me that Phoebe isn't sharing the whole truth—that she and Millard are not nearly as happily married as she lets on—but I also recognize that I have pushed the matter far enough for one afternoon. I continue shoveling, and after a respectable pause, I ask, "So what's with the spider?"

"What?"

"I realize that it's probably none of my business, but your son carries a giant plastic spider with him everywhere he goes," I say. "Don't tell me you haven't noticed."

I could care less about spiders, of course. But I have learned that nothing soothes—or distracts—a woman more than talking about her own children.

"You know how it is with kids and phases," replies Phoebe, but she is gazing into the low-hanging sky, as though her son's arachnid obsession is a manifestation of divine will, and I sense that her thoughts are entirely elsewhere. "Oliver is a good kid," she muses. "Smart too. He takes after his father. Both of my children do." Then—without any warning—Phoebe asks, "What are your plans for the summer?"

Now she has caught *me* off guard. Over the past few days, as I've watched the undergraduates sledding down Founder's Hill, I've managed to forget that classes will let out in three weeks and the campus will once again drift into slumber. At one time, I had been planning to spend my months off cultivating daylilies, and driving out to my sister's lake house on weekends, but Ellen's unheated mountain cabin now seems far less inviting.

"I suppose I'll do some sunbathing," I quip. "Maybe I'll host a barbecue for July 4th."

Phoebe does not smile. "We're not staying here," she announces. "Millard is arranging a teaching gig in Florida for July. He has a close friend at Tampa State. If they really do shut the university down early, we might leave by the end of next week."

"But you're coming back in the fall."

Phoebe shrugs. "It was forty-two degrees yesterday in Tampa. Not exactly beach weather, but better than permafrost."

"You can't be serious," I say. "You just got here."

"We've been here *all semester*," she says—which is apparently the truth. "Jesus, William. It's not as though I didn't exist before you ran into me." Phoebe takes a deep breath and clasps her bare hand inside her gloved one. "Look, I'm sorry. I didn't mean to snap at you like that," she adds. "It's just that I'm reaching my breaking point. I shouldn't be telling you this, but I was too upset to get out of bed yesterday."

"Is there anything I can do?"

"Not unless you have a private stash of heating oil," says Phoebe. "Last night, the temperature *inside* my house wasn't even forty-two degrees. If we don't figure something out soon, I'm going to have to send the kids to stay with my mother-in-law so they don't freeze to death while they're sleeping. Do you understand how humiliating that is?" In an uncharacteristic burst of scorn, Phoebe hisses like a feral cat and makes an aggressive, clawing motion with her naked hand—as though she wants to gouge blood from the atmosphere. "The woman appeared in two B-movies fifty years ago. *Two*. But from the way she issues orders, you'd think she was Greta Garbo."

I bite my lower lip to keep from smirking: So now I know where Millard has acquired his Hollywood airs. What I really want to ask Phoebe is why she married this pretentious folklorist with the overbearing mother? What did *he* have that *I* didn't? Was it all about his imperial forehead and unyielding jaw-line? But I suppose that's like explaining why some tropical waves swell into cyclones, while others ripple to harmless spray, and even if Phoebe could explain her choice, experience has taught me that women grow uncharacteristically evasive when you pry into the mechanics of their marriages. Since I have no insights to offer on the subject of in-laws—that's one of the few humiliations I have yet to suffer—I confine my response to a benevolent frown and a sympathetic nod.

"The snow is letting up," I observe hopefully. "Maybe we're in for a warm spell."

I lean my shovel against the retaining wall and admire my handi-work. I've cleared more than enough space for a car to pull up the drive. All around us, the world is white and still and cold—a planet swaddled in a vast and lifeless silence. Only the occasional chatter of chickadees in the basswoods holds out any promise of renewal.

"This was fun," I say. "We should do this again tomorrow."

"Should we?" asks Phoebe—her spirits apparently lifted. "What happened to that warm spell you just promised me?"

"On the off chance it snows tomorrow," I correct myself, "we should do this again."

"Tomorrow, *on the off chance it snows*," she answers, shaking her head as though admonishing a wayward child, "I'm going to hire a high school kid with a snow-blower to do the entire job in ten minutes... and you're going to be too sore to scratch your own nose."

She has a point. I can already sense my forearms stiffening. I think of the teenager who will earn twenty easy bucks for clearing Phoebe's driveway in the morning—who may yet have an opportunity to escort his own Phoebe Marboe to the senior prom—and I yearn to be that adolescent boy so much that my eyes sting from the tears.

· · · · ·

The warm spell that I have promised Phoebe does not come to pass. What greets us the following dawn is a vicious Alberta clipper that seals the snow pack beneath several inches of slick and impenetrable ice. Chancellor Endicott had called an emergency meeting of the tenured faculty for ten o'clock—to discuss pruning the final three weeks off the spring semester—but conditions are so poor that even this summit must be postponed to the afternoon. When the hour for the rescheduled conclave finally does arrive, Trask Amphitheater is filled to capacity. I see faces I haven't laid eyes upon since I was a post-doc—and one wizened member of our own department, emeritus for decades, who I'd honestly believed to be dead.

While we wait for the provost to upload his computer presentation—the man has fifty slides for us on the economic dangers of keeping the university's doors open—the buzz among my colleagues is confined to only one subject: the weather. Will temperatures really stay below zero for the remainder of the week? Did the halo around last night's moon mean we're in for more storms? Is it true that the cattle on the agriculture campus are all facing west for the first time in modern memory? And what should be made of the sudden influx of ravens? I find these conversations indescribably refreshing. In the days before professional forecasting, the divining of sunshine and squalls formed the crux of communal life and the basis of countless friendships. I can still remember my own dear grandmother opining, *When windows won't open and salt clogs the shaker, the weather will favor the umbrella maker*, which is conditionally true, and, *Cats and dogs eat grass before a rain*, which is patently false. So while I am grateful for Mesoscale modeling—I've spent my entire adult life in its thrall—my stomach flutters when I hear the beak-nosed woman behind me tell her mousy colleague that *if clouds move against the wind, rain will follow*, even though, at a scientific level, this aphorism is sheer twaddle.

After assuring the conclave that an early closing will not affect salaries or benefits, the provost calls for a show of hands. I vote to keep the university open. So does another member of my department, a junior paleontologist from Barrow, Alaska. I spot a third raised hand in the balcony, but upon further inquiry, it turns out the owner is merely stretching. So by a vote of everyone-to-two, the university decides to suspend classes in forty-eight hours. Professors will be responsible for determining their own grading schemes in the absence of final exams. A consolidation of office space will take place at a later date, for those faculty wishing to remain on campus, to save on both heating costs and security. (Looting has already broken out at several New England boarding schools after they've shuttered their dorms for the summer.) After three hundred years of scholarship, education in Laurendale has come to a grinding halt.

I'm already in the coffee shop of the ground floor, about to indulge my caffeine habit, when Phoebe's husband catches up with

me. He's sporting a broad-shouldered overcoat, a fuchsia silk shirt
with a mandarin collar, and an aviator scarf, all of which combine
to give him the petty, buffoonish appearance of a civil servant in a
Gilbert and Sullivan operetta.

"Professor Deutsch, right?" he asks. "The global cooling fellow?"

"I like to think of myself as a climatologist," I reply dryly.

"Sure, a climatologist," he agrees. "Millard Alexander. Folklore."

"I didn't even know we *had* a folklore department," I say.

"We *do* and I teach in it," he answers, not even remotely flustered. "Which is why I wanted to have a brief word with you. Do
you have a moment?"

"Actually," I lie, "I'm late for a conference."

I wish I could slide past Alexander and vanish, but I haven't yet
paid for my coffee. Under different circumstances, I would drop a
dollar bill on the checkout counter—escaping Phoebe's husband
is worth fifteen cents change—but this afternoon the clerk is the
blind work-study student who relies on the good faith of her cli-
ents. I'm afraid that if I try to sneak away, the other patrons may
think I'm cheating the helpless girl. All I can do is inch my way
toward the checkout line while keeping my eyes on the folklorist.

"I assure you I won't take much of your time," he says. "Here's
my question: nearly all of the cultures of Europe share a common
myth—not so different from our Groundhog Day—that the weather
on a particular date can be used to forecast for the weeks to come.
Saint Swithun's Day in Britain. Saint Médard's Feast in France. Saint
Godelieve's Day in Belgium. The Celebration of the Protecting Veil
in Russia. So I couldn't help wondering, Professor Deutsch, since so
many different societies profess versions of the same myth, whether
these prophesies might have some grounding in scientific reality."

If a hidden agenda lurks within this inquiry, I cannot decipher
it. I had expected the folklorist's request to be overtly allegori-

cal—maybe an inquiry about Icarus soaring too close to the sun, or a sermon disguised as a query about the links between moon cycles and infidelity—but Phoebe's husband comes across as earnest and ineffably polite. Still, I find Millard Alexander's company intolerable. He strikes me as a man who has never truly suffered in life—not as Phoebe or I have suffered—and I've always felt it was internal torment that separates a society's wheat from its chaff.

"I doubt there is any empirical basis for those myths," I say. "Human beings have been trying to explain the weather for a darn long time—and, if we've learned nothing else this past week, it's that most of us still aren't very good at it."

"I suspected as much," he says, "but I had to ask."

"Of course, you did."

Alexander extends his hand and I shake it—but he does not immediately let go.

"One more thing, Professor Deutsch," he says. "Stay away from my wife."

The folklorist's hand—strong and bony—is still clutching mine. He could easily break my fingers with more pressure.

"I am sure I don't understand," I say.

"*I'm sure you do,*" he says icily. "I am warning you, Professor Deutsch. If I catch you anywhere near Phoebe, I won't be responsible for what happens."

· · · · ·

That night we set the all-time low for Laurendale. Not the all-time low *for the date*, but a bone-snapping -31° that marks the second lowest temperature ever recorded south of the Mason-Dixon Line. We're at the point where children lose fingers after thirty-second exposures and automobile engines freeze solid on public streets, so I am grateful that the ignition in my Buick turns over on the first attempt. Far more challenging is the drive across town, because all of the traffic lights have succumbed to the chill—and, even in a Southern college town, what good Samaritan is going to risk frostbite to direct traffic by hand? Fortunately, I don't have to lecture this morning—nobody does anymore—so there isn't any need to be at the university at an early hour. The truth of the matter is that there is no need to visit campus *at all*—I could easily run my computer simulations from home—except that I'm hoping to reap another improvised encounter with Phoebe. Needless to say, I cannot adequately convey the intensity of the sinking throb that I experience as I am cruising up Chickahominy Boulevard, when I spot the Steinhoff & Son moving truck parked at the head of the Alexanders' block. Two ski-masked creatures in chin-to-toe coveralls—you can hardly discern that human beings hide beneath these shapeless husks of synthetic fiber—are hoisting a credenza up the vehicle's plywood gangway.

My first impulse is to bolt up the slate steps and to plead with Phoebe not to leave Laurendale, but as long as Millard Alexander remains inside the house, or until I am certain that he has already departed, all that I can do is burn through my fuel reserves while the movers cart off loveseats and bureaus and sheet-draped wall-mirrors. The spectacle reminds me of the grainy footage of World War I refugees that we watched in high school, so many years before, the Belgian families crossing the Marne Bridge with feather beds loaded atop horse-drawn wagons. My dashboard thermometer is worthless these days—it bottoms out at -5° Fahrenheit—but a white sun breaks through the cloud-cover around noon, and rays of pure light glisten off the rolling, drift-skinned lawns. By this point, I've already been waiting three hours, so I'm seriously thinking about jettisoning what remains of my good judgment and ringing Phoebe's doorbell—although an uninvited house call, especially with her husband at home, will raise the stakes between us multiple notches. Hour by hour, I throw down proverbial gauntlets for myself in the snow: I'll ring the bell when three more cars pass on Patrick Henry Street, when the Evensong service concludes at the Episcopal Chapel. But much like I did as a teenager—when I repeatedly promised myself that I would ask out Phoebe on a certain yet ever-sliding date—I now allow one deadline to melt into another. Then around four o'clock, shortly after the postman makes his rounds on cross-country skis, Millard Alexander steps out onto the veranda. The folklorist surveys the block like a whaler scanning the horizon for flumes—and for a fleeting moment I'm certain his gaze locks me in its sights—but he must be staring right past me, I think, because he pulls his jacket tight around his neck and strides rapidly toward the main quadrangle. I suppose this is the sign that I've been searching for: I take a deep breath and—as soon as the folklorist disappears behind a stand of lindens—I mount the porch of the Victorian.

Phoebe answers the door in an angora sweater, insulated cargo pants and plush earmuffs. She does not appear at all surprised to see me. "Come inside quickly," she urges. "Before the warm air escapes." I want to ask: *What warm air?* The Alexanders' foyer has been stripped of all furnishings, except for a child's rocking horse, and my professional estimate places the temperature south of twenty-five degrees. Before I have time to ask about the heat, Phoebe leads me into a second room—an equally barren parlor where an active fireplace generates just enough warmth to make its occupancy tolerable—and she shuts the door firmly behind us. I make instant note of the unusual kindling: splintered table legs and bookshelves, a supply of which remains stockpiled around the hearth. My companion sits down unceremoniously on the shag carpet, so I do the same.

"You've been watching the house, haven't you?" Phoebe asks.

"Only for a little while," I lie. "I've been waiting for your husband to leave."

Phoebe nods. "Millard cleared out intentionally. He said he wanted to give me a few hours on my own, before we left, to take care of any private business that I had," she says. "I have no idea what you said to him yesterday, but he came home last night insisting that we couldn't spend another weekend in Virginia." Phoebe folded her arms across her chest, rubbing her shivering sleeves for warmth. "I've *never* seen Millard so worked up."

"Where are your kids?"

"At their grandmother's," says Phoebe, in a high-pitched voice dripping with mimicry and sarcasm. "Grandma Eve's building has enough heating oil to roast a fucking iceberg." She clears her throat and adds, "In case you're wondering, *we* ran out."

The flames behind the grill reflect off the floor tiles around the edges of the throw rug and cast lambent tongues over Phoebe's pastel cheeks. We are sitting only feet apart—so close that I could easily wrap my arms around her waist, sheltering her warmth with my own—only I fear that she will push me away, that she might prefer to remain alone in the cold. I can't help thinking that she's still a stunning beauty, even packaged in mohair. That's when I realize the miniature cavalry charge in the background is the chattering of her teeth.

"You're freezing," I observe. "Where's your coat?"

"I gave it to Meghan," she says. "Millard's mother invited me to stay with her too, but I didn't have it in me. Now I'm having second thoughts."

I would give her my own coat, of course, but I don't think she'd accept it.

"I was thinking about you last night," she says. "And it finally came back to me. You were *Billy* with the stutter—and you used to park that ancient Plymouth of yours across the street and stare at our house on weekend nights." Phoebe doesn't sound upset, or even amused—merely matter-of-fact. "I guess I blocked all of that out. I don't like to think about my childhood very often—*at all*, really—not if I can help it."

"I was a ridiculous kid, wasn't I?"

Phoebe smiles. "I think it was sweet. Adorable, really." The look she offers me is one of genuine warmth and affection. "I don't know why I wouldn't date you then. *I should have.* If I could do it over again, I'd like to think I *would* go out with you."

I can tell by her tone that a door is closing, not opening—but I've already come so far.

"And now?" I ask. "It's not too late."

"And now," says Phoebe, "I'm moving to Tampa, Florida. I have two children who depend on me, and a husband willing to let me take care of my private business without throwing any plates or phoning a divorce lawyer. My husband isn't a bad guy, William. After growing up with a father like mine, there's a lot to be said for a man who steers with an even keel." She stands up suddenly and adjusts the burning "logs" with a poker, generating a flurry of sparks. "I heard on the news what you said about time," she says. "I found it very eloquent."

I stand up and step behind her. "So this is goodbye?"

"I guess it is," she says.

I know that if I remain so close to her for another moment, I will reach out for her body, and there is the possibility she might reach back—even though this is not what she desires. Instead, I unbutton my coat and quickly drape it over her shoulders. She turns, but already I'm retreating toward the entryway.

"You'll get sick," she cries.

"I have another one," I answer. "At home."

I cross the foyer without looking back and step out into the frigid summer air. A solemn peace blankets the white landscape. The sun hangs low in the sky, but it is not yet gone. I do not have another overcoat at home, of course, but I am determined to acclimate to the chill—to prove myself a match for the cold. Enough time will pass, I assure myself, and even the memories of mild springs will fade. We will no longer speak nostalgically of the golden era before the temperature dropped, of the balmy days preceding those first May flurries or the joy a man once felt climbing through his office window into an afternoon festooned with snow. The frost will be all we've ever known, all we've ever had, so we will manage to endure it, convincing ourselves that life could not be any other way.

Invasive Species

· ·

While her daughter practices for the afterlife—Celeste's tumor-frayed body waiting rigid inside the case of the grandfather clock—Meredith watches their new neighbor hacking at the undergrowth with a machete. This is the fifth morning in a row that the lanky, white-haired retiree has been lopping the heads off vines, slaughtering some plants and sparing others according to an algorithm Meredith can't decipher. At first, she'd mistaken the knife for a scythe. In his dungarees and black hooded sweatshirt, the long-faced man looks like the Grim Reaper on his day off. But also handsome, in an odd way. So when he waves a gloved hand at Meredith over the azalea hedge, and then strolls toward her across the unkempt yard, she feels a genuine twinge of nervous anticipation. Immediately, she stifles these thoughts: This man is old enough to have diapered her. And her daughter is dying. Imminently! What business does she have imagining a romantic life beyond her mourning?

The man climbs the patio stairs slowly, bracing himself against the iron railing. A brutal wince crosses his face, but quickly vanishes. "I'm Cohan. Scotch-Irish, not Jewish," he says. "I thought I'd take a breather and say hello."

"Well, hello," says Meredith. She smiles, but trains her gaze on the ice cube in her lemonade glass. "I'm Meredith Eycke. Jewish,

Irish, German, Dutch, Serbo-Croatian and Lord-knows-what-else. Probably kangaroo and flamingo mixed in."

"Kangaroo and flamingo," echoes Cohan. "Kangamingo."

Meredith looks up at him from the chaise lounge. His large dark eyes glisten with insight, or possibly mischief, and his voice carries a hint of the ocean. He lights a pipe, and the sweet tobacco scent floats on the moist autumn air.

"You're fighting the woods," says Meredith.

"Invasive species," he answers. "Chinese wisteria, periwinkle, garlic mustard. If George Washington rode across the Virginia of today, he'd hardly recognize the place." Cohan pauses, as though any mention of President Washington warrants reverence. He gazes toward the densely-forested hillside. "That's why I bought out here. I can't bring back the entire pre-Columbian habitat, but the least I can do is restore an acre and a half. When you reach my age, you can't help think about these things. About your legacy."

This is how a man should be, she thinks. Effortlessly confident. Knowledgeable of history and the natural world. Yet also quixotic, in an endearing way, about his occasional backyard project. She glances at the clock, unsure whether she should retrieve her daughter. *Her legacy.* Celeste has been playing dead for more than an hour.

"All of our ecosystems are out of whack," explains Cohan. "That's what my generation has done. In Guam, non-native tree snakes cause daily power outages; coqui frogs on Hawaii produce infestations louder than jumbo jets—" He cuts himself off abruptly. "I'm sorry. I get carried away."

"No, I was interested," says Meredith. "It's amazing how much is going on in the world that I know nothing about."

Their eyes meet—and lock for a twinkling. An acknowledgement, maybe, that this visit is more than neighborly. That Cohan of the

Scotch-Irish Cohans will drop by again. Then he grins sheepishly, as though he has just remembered an off-color joke, and his gaze darts across the patio. The clock stands beside the bay windows, beneath an overhanging eave, but its trunk is plastered with damp yellow leaves. "Interesting place for a clock," observes Cohan with a forced offhandedness. "I suppose your husband refurbishes antiques."

"Oh. I don't have a husband," she answers. Too zealously. "My daughter likes hiding in there, so I paid a couple of high school boys to lug it outside. To get her some fresh air...I know that sounds even crazier than it is."

"Not at all. I used to be a kid shrink." Now that he has discovered that she's unmarried, Cohan allows his eyes to linger over her body—on her ample, 47-year-old breasts, and her fleshy, childbearing hips. It has been many years since anybody has looked at Meredith with such blatant appetite. Cohan takes an indulgent drag on his pipe, breaths out a plume of smoke, and ambles to the door of the clock. "May I?"

Meredith nods.

The clock is oak cross-banded with mahogany, an eighteenth century masterpiece by Gillett of Manchester. Its trunk is large enough to fit an entire family. Meredith often hid beneath the pendulum as a child. So when she sold off the inventory from her father's shop—six decades of expertise reduced to an overstuffed showroom on a neglected Richmond side street—this was the one treasure she'd kept.

Cohan stands nearly as tall as the swan-necks atop the frame, and he has to stoop to pull on the tiny brass door-handle. Inside, Celeste sits in self-imposed rigor mortis: eyes clenched, fists balled, teeth locked in a ghoulish grin. She is bundled into a wool sweater—a single, hard-fought concession to the exigencies of being alive. The late afternoon sun makes her pale, hairless scalp appear practically translucent, exposing the latticework of slender blood vessels that carry the metastases through her body like a miniature plumbing system.

Cohan is clearly surprised by her daughter's appearance, but he doesn't betray any discomfort. "Do you live in here, young lady?" he asks—neither patronizing nor ironic. Just intensely sincere. Meredith decides she could love this man.

"You can't come in," says Celeste. "This is only for dead people."

"Are you dead?" asks Cohan.

"Nope. But I will be soon, so I'm practicing. Protesilaus is showing me how."

"Protesilaus?"

"He's my friend. He was killed in Ancient Greece."

"Ancient Greece," says Cohan—his voice filling with awe. "Is Protesilaus real?"

"Uh-huh," says Celeste, nodding vigorously. "He's a very good teacher."

"Are you *sure* he's real?"

"Okay, he's not *really* real," whispers Celeste. "But don't tell him, or you'll hurt his feelings."

· · · · ·

The next morning, Celeste announces that she wants to learn how to tell time. This is obviously a fruitless exercise—the child will be dead in a month or two—but Meredith is ecstatic. Not since they called off the chemo has her daughter shown enthusiasm for anything other than "death practice." So if the girl wants to learn how to read a watch—or a sundial—how can Meredith not be grateful?

But the prospect isn't without its ghosts. When Meredith was a child, she yearned to unlock the mysteries of analog time the way her older brother hankered for the keys to the family Plymouth. Each birthday passed with increasing responsibilities: removing and polishing the delicate wooden birds that nested in the cuckoo clocks; tightening the mainspring of the Willard lighthouse model with its silver-and-ruby-handled winding key. On Meredith's eighth birthday, her mother revealed to her the rudiments of hours and minutes on a well-worn banjo-style clock-front than had been severed from its internal gears. Thelma Eycke called it "a face without a brain." But that night, Mrs. Eycke choked to death on a lamb chop during a Chamber of Commerce dinner, and so it was Celeste's narcoleptic grand-aunt who eventually taught her how brief moments combine into lengthy intervals: on a plastic toy purchased at Woolworth's.

This week, unfortunately, the local stores don't have any toy time-pieces in stock. It seems there has been a run on plastic watches and owl-shaped clock faces—maybe in conjunction with the time-telling portion of the third grade curriculum. Meredith phones everyone she knows within driving distance in search of the proper device. This is not many people. She works from home, designing schedules for professional sports leagues and concert venues. Her older brother is dead. Her nieces and nephews have scattered. Eventually, another mother from her pediatric cancer support group, whose twin eleven-year-old boys both suffer from neuroblastomas, offers her a talking clock-telephone combo. The contraption is manufactured by Walt Disney, so the six and twelve on the face are cartoons of Donald Duck and Pluto. When you set the time, the console rings. When you pick up the receiver, a mechanized voice announces the hour and minute. Celeste is a swift learner, and soon she imitates the voice with impressive accuracy.

"You're a natural time-teller," says Meredith. "Grandpa would be proud."

"That's why I'm learning," answers Celeste. "To show Grandpa. I asked him to teach me how last night, but he said he'd forgotten. It's hard to remember how clocks work when you're dead."

"You saw your grandfather *yesterday*?" This is not so much a question as an acknowledgement. Meredith remains unsure how far to indulge her daughter's make-believe afterlife. According to the oncologist, such highly-developed delusions are rare—even as a coping mechanism. But what harm can they do, right?

"Grandpa said to say hi," says Celeste. "He misses you."

"I miss him too," says Meredith.

"In heaven, he's married to Helen of Troy."

Several months earlier, before she'd left school, Celeste had come home from "reading hour" at the library with a copy of *Bulfinch's Mythology for Children*. All of her afterlife fantasies now featured heroes of antiquity.

"What about Grandma?" asks Meredith—a bit defensive.

This puzzles the girl, at first. She squints and purses her lips, but then laughs. "He's married to Grandma *too*," says Celeste. "It's okay, Mama. The rules are different in heaven."

Meredith does not believe in heaven. She believes life is a one-way trip from naught to oblivion. If there were an afterlife—if there were a God—the sperm they'd given her at the fertility center would have been pristine as mountain snow, not tainted with a roadmap for galloping tumors. Ever since she has driven out to Petersburg to retrieve the talking clock, she has been thinking about the mother of the twins. What will the woman feel if one survives, but the other does not. Will she be thankful? Devastated? Merely bewildered? Where Meredith's father had come from— Jewish Rotterdam, before the war—a mother was *lucky* to have one of two children survive to adulthood.

Celeste slides the minute hand over the hour hand, so that both face downward. "What time is it?" she asks. It is unclear whether she means the artificial time of the toy clock, or the real time of the living world.

"Six thirty," says Meredith.

"Exactly?"

"Exactly."

"How many seconds?"

The toy clock has no second hand. This sounds like one of those mind-taunting questions that fascinate children and philosophers: Do the seconds exist, if there is no tool to measure them? Meredith knows that a father couldn't solve these mysteries any better than she can, but still—! Instinctively, she looks for Cohan out at the fringe of their yards, where exurban civilization meets the modern wilderness, but either he has taken an early lunch break or he has immersed himself fully in the undergrowth.

"It's hard to measure seconds," says Meredith. "They go by too quickly."

"Nine seconds," says Celeste. "Six thirty and nine seconds. Protesilaus predicted that would be the time when I asked."

"Nine seconds, then," agrees Meredith.

"Protesilaus was killed in the Trojan War. Because he was brave and got off his warship first," explains Celeste. "His wife, Laodamia, was allowed to visit him. But for just three hours. She was the only mortal ever allowed to visit a dead person."

Meredith hears Cohan before she sees him. He has climbed up the side stairs of the patio, carrying a ripe pumpkin as large as a horse's head. The narrow, oblong shape of the pumpkin makes it appear unhappy. "What about Orpheus?" Cohan asks. "Didn't Orpheus go to Hades to visit Eurydice?"

Celeste considers this. "Maybe he did," she says. "And maybe he didn't."

"That's a fair answer," agrees Cohan. He sets the pumpkin down on the picnic table. "Do you think Protesilaus would like to help carve a jack-o-lantern?"

"I'll ask him," says Celeste, "next time I see him."

"Would *you* like to carve a jack-o-lantern?" he asks.

"I don't know," she answers.

Cohan reaches into the pocket of his parka—like a magician rummaging for a rabbit—and retrieves a black felt-tipped marker. He follows this up with an eight-piece set of carving tools bound in a worn leather case. They are heirlooms, he explains. A Christmas present from his own father. Celeste draws matching faces—one joyful, one sad—on either side of the pumpkin. "It's Janus, the doorway god," she says. With Cohan's help, she cuts round eyes, then both square and triangular teeth.

While he supervises Celeste's carving, Cohan talks to Meredith about the ecology of species introduction. "Today, we've come to view invasives as a threat, but that hasn't always been the case. A hundred years ago, acclimation societies intentionally transplanted European fauna to America. House sparrows, pigeons. One group with a literary bent tried to bring over all the birds in Shakespeare's plays." Cohan steers Celeste's hand while he speaks, showing the girl to chisel *away* from her body. A flock of songbirds settles in the crabapple branches overhead. "Speaking of the devil," says Cohan. "Those are the starlings that are out-competing our native bluebirds."

"You know an awful lot about invasive species," says Meredith.

"I guess I do," he answers. Clearly delighted. "Life leads a man down strange paths. As recently as March of last year, believe it or not, I didn't know the first thing about ecology. I hardly knew the difference between a flamingo and a kangaroo . . . I didn't become serious about invasives until my wife passed on . . ."

"I'm sorry," says Meredith.

But she is also pleased. That he is a widower. That he has not abandoned the mother of his children, or grown old and peculiar in bachelordom.

"I'm sorry too," says Cohan. "She was a true gem of a woman."

He cups his chin and stares absently toward the far end of the patio—past the skeletons of forsythia and honeysuckle, beyond the mail-order Langstroth hives, where Meredith's other neighbor, Dr. Seward, has taken up beekeeping. Celeste peels away an eyebrow of pumpkin skin. "What did your wife look like?" she asks.

A hush descends on the patio, broken only by the honk of distant geese. Cohan looks at Celeste with wonder, blinking, as though he has discovered a new species.

"Darlene? Honestly, she looked like an exotic vase," he finally answers. "She had the most perfect slender neck, and a waist so slim I could wrap my arm all the way around it."

"If I meet her when I'm dead," Celeste offers, "I'll say hi for you."

Cohan stands up on his stiff knees. "When Darlene took sick," he says to Meredith, "I found it very helpful to slash up unwanted vegetation. To let loose. If you ever want to join me, there are enough invasives out there for both of us."

"I'll think about it," she agrees.

"It would be a help, in fact. I'd like to clear the place out before Thanksgiving."

He walks to the edge of the flagstone deck and Meredith follows, though it almost feels as though he is drawing her with him. When he reaches the stairs, he pauses on the first step and turns around. They are now the same height. An ideal height to embrace or rub noses. Instead, he places his arm on her shoulder with great tenderness. "I know this isn't my business," he asks, "but have you made any plans?"

She knows exactly what he means.

"I promised her she'd stay at home," says Meredith. "We have a nurse coming. We'll have a morphine drip up in her bedroom."

"That's good," says Cohan. "Home is *always* good."

"It's very kind of you to take such an interest in Celeste," says Meredith. "I wish I could thank you."

"You're assuming I don't have an ulterior motive," says Cohan.

The widower doesn't give Meredith an opportunity to respond. (And she is grateful for this, because she's sure she'd have said the wrong thing.) Instead, he brushes the side of her upper sleeve with his fingertips, like a Near Eastern merchant examining a rare fabric, and then vanishes under the wisteria arbor and around the side of his gardening shed.

Celeste, meanwhile, has completed her carving. She lugs the jack-o-lantern to Meredith—hugging it in her frail, wasted arms. "I lied to Mr. Cohan about Protesilaus not being real," the girl says, as though she has been thinking over this confession all day long. "That's called humoring."

. . . . .

The need for the visiting nurse arrives much sooner than Meredith expects. That evening, Celeste is too fatigued to help set the dinner table. She pokes at her lasagna, running her fork through the marinara sauce like a plow. Meredith toasts her daughter a Pop-Tart, hoping this will tempt her, but Celeste pushes away the plate. Meredith considers bribing her to eat—she'd give anything she had if the girl would just swallow one thin slice of banana—but what can one offer an eight-year-old girl with only weeks to live? By the following morning, the child is so worn down that she needs assistance putting on her overalls. She denies being in pain, but Meredith doesn't believe her. Her nearly perpetual smile begins to looks more like a grimace.

"I'm going to call for the nurse," Meredith says.

"Can you carry me downstairs first?" Celeste asks. "I want to practice."

"I don't know how good an idea that is, darling," she objects. "It's getting awfully chilly out."

"But there's no temperature when you're dead," Celeste explains. Her tone is something between bemused and frustrated—like a teenager arguing with a parent who doesn't get it. Who *never* gets it. "I *need* to practice, Mama. It will be much harder to be dead if I'm unprepared."

So Meredith swaddles her daughter in a heavy hand-knit quilt—so snug that only her sunken eyes show—and lifts the child into her arms. Outside, the air has turned much cooler; a brisk wind rattles the birdfeeders and slaps a maple branch against the aluminum siding. When Meredith places the child's paper-light body into the trunk of the clock, it feels as though she's lowering an infant into a coffin. But what choice does she have? "It's good practice for you too, Mama," says Celeste. "This way you won't be so lonely when I leave. You can just pretend I'm in the clock."

The visiting nurse, Maricel, doesn't see it that way, of course. She's a round-faced Filipino woman, somewhere between thirty-five and fifty, with a double chin and wisps of coarse dark hair around her ears. Her Celtic cross pendant is set with a tiny red garnet. When she shuffles through the house, she moans softly with each step as though her shoes don't fit properly. Meredith wonders if the woman has children of her own, but that's a hard question past a certain age.

"She'll have to come inside, Mrs. Eycke," says Maricel. "I can't look after a girl locked in a cabinet."

"Is it such a big deal?" asks Meredith. "She's happy out there."

Meredith is tempted to add: Odysseus and Agamemnon live in the clock. But she realizes this is not something the nurse will understand. Having a stranger in the house makes her nervous: it has been nearly a year since she has had company. Nearly a year since

Celeste's diagnosis. Dishes are piled high in the sink. Odds and ends are strewn across the kitchen table: a half-pack of birthday candles, a Phillips-head screwdriver, old shower curtain rings. Dust balls fringe the chair legs in the dining room. While she negotiates with the nurse, Meredith straightens picture frames and Windexes down the refrigerator door. As though this is all part of her daily housework routine. Deep down, she knows Maricel is an employee. Not a social caller. But Meredith has never before had an employee—the very idea makes her neck sweat—so she offers the nurse tea and Irish soda bread. She serves on her mother's good china, the hand-painted porcelain teacups with the pinkie-sized handles.

"You're not Jehovah's Witnesses?" asks the nurse.

"I don't know what we are," says Meredith. "But we're not that."

Maricel pours another packet of Sweet'N Low into her tea. She has also added nearly a cow's worth of milk, topping off the cup after each sip. "I've looked after Witness children a couple of times. It's always an adventure," she says. "I figured that might be why you have the girl in the clock. Something wacky-religious."

"She *wants* to sit in the clock," says Meredith defensively. The possibility crosses her mind, for the first time, that this woman could report her for neglect. *Abuse*. How would it sound explaining to a family court judge why she'd abandoned a terminally-ill eight-year-old to the November frost? Meredith glances out the window: snowflakes are falling like tiny artificial feathers.

"She doesn't know what she wants. She's eight years old," says Maricel confidently. "She needs to be told what she wants."

So together they retrieve Celeste from the clock. Meredith's daughter is more animated than she was earlier, red-faced and almost energetic, but now she admits that her back hurts. And her abdomen. And the base of her skull. The pain is so severe that some-times it blocks out her thoughts. She's perfectly willing to lean on her mother's arm and walk to her bedroom.

Maricel tucks the girl under the covers, then deftly hooks her right arm up to the I.V. Meredith holds her daughter's opposite hand. She looks away as the needle slides in, but she smells the sharpness of the rubbing alcohol. Once the line has taken, the nurse gives the girl a second injection.

"Tell Mr. Cohan that his wife sends him a humungous hug," says Celeste. She closes her eyes. "Mrs. Cohan is very pretty. But you're prettier, Mama."

"Thank you," says Meredith.

"That should knock her out for a few hours," says the nurse. "I always start off with a strong dose. Sometimes that catches the pain by surprise."

"This is all happening faster than I expected," says Meredith.

"Sometimes if you surprise the pain, it goes into hiding," explains the nurse, nodding and fussing with Celeste's pillows. "Maybe you'd like to lie down too, Mrs. Eycke? So you'll be awake when your daughter is…"

"Maybe," agrees Meredith.

She wanders into the hallway, but doesn't take a nap. Instead, she sits at the kitchen table, staring through the glass door at the Gillett of Manchester. A film of snow has settled over the antique wood. Meredith remembers the first time she wound the grandfather clock—how she turned the giant key, then hid inside the base and listened to the grind and thump of the gears. Already, at the age of eight, she knew the truth about clocks: how they pretend that time goes on forever, when it really stops abruptly. All it takes is a lamb chop, or one small cell gone haywire.

She senses the doorbell has rung several times, before she's aware enough to answer it. Hours have gone by; it's nearly nightfall. Cohan is standing on the back steps, wearing a bright orange knit cap with a tassel and a matching scarf. He carries a brown paper bag under one arm—like a suitor presenting a bottle of wine on a first date. When Meredith opens the door, an icy blast gusts into the kitchen and billows under the drapes.

Cohan steps into the house and dusts the flurries off his shoulders.

"How's the patient?" he asks.

Meredith smiles. Cohan's hat makes him look goofy, but loveable. "She's calm," says Meredith. "Calmer than I am."

"I didn't see you outside," says Cohan. "I figured . . ."

She nods. "I'm bad with the nurse. I don't think she likes me."

"You're just paranoid," says Cohan. "How could anybody not like you?"

Three days, thinks Meredith. I've known you *three days.* But Cohan speaks as though they've been close friends since childhood.

"I could be paranoid and she could *still* not like me," says Meredith. "I read something like that once on a T-shirt."

Cohan grins—but she senses it is a false grin.

"Look," he says. His voice is serious now. "I've brought you something."

He hands her the bag. It's very light. *Not* a bottle of champagne.

"This is an invasive weed from Thailand. It's for the end—it will make things go quicker, if you want that. Better than morphine." Cohan stuffs his empty hands into his trouser pockets. He appears less sure of himself—like a schoolboy second-guessing a prank. "All you do is boil the root in hot water and have her drink the extract."

"Oh, Jesus," says Meredith.

"Only if you want it," repeats Cohan.

"Okay," says Meredith.

"And when you're ready," he adds, "you come outside and we'll hack some invasives together. Sound good?"

"Okay," she says again.

Meredith clutches the paper bag to her chest while Cohan backs his way out the door and into the night. Instinctively, she conceals the package from the nurse.

"I heard a visitor," says Maricel. "I didn't want to interrupt."

Meredith wonders how long this woman has been listening.

"He's a very handsome man," says the nurse. "He looks like a doctor."

"He was a doctor," says Meredith.

Maricel clicks her tongue against her palate in disapproval. "When I lecture to the nursing students, that's the most important lesson I teach them: never trust a good-looking doctor. He's bound to be your undoing."

Is this a warning? A threat? Meredith and the nurse stare at each other across the dimly-lit kitchen. Then Maricel laughs—a warm, raucous laugh. "It's certainly been my undoing," she says. "And let me tell you: I wouldn't mind being undone again."

. . . . .

At first, she isn't sure whether to be appreciative or angry. He's a peculiar man, this Arthur Cohan, who devotes his golden years to eradicating knapweed and chinaberries. And he has given her a lethal herb for her daughter—knowing full well that she could turn him in to the authorities, placing his own future entirely in her power. Not that she will ever use the poison. Of course not. But Meredith admits there is a solace in knowing it exists, stashed on a back shelf in the pantry behind a tin that once held imported Danish cookies. She checks on the root several times a day. To make sure it is there. Maybe because it keeps her from going out into the yard.

Cohan pays her no more visits. She can see him through the window of her daughter's bedroom. He looks smaller from the

second story, more a part of the landscape, like a Russian peas-
ant in one of those nineteenth century novels. He has traded in
his machete for a shovel, and he digs at assorted roots. A metallic
object catches the sunlight in the nearby grass, and Meredith realizes this is a second shovel. Cohan is waiting for her to join him.
But she knows what this means, because as irrational as it is, the
man has planted the idea in her head: if she goes to work beside
her neighbor, she'll have to accept that her daughter really will die.

Celeste drifts in and out of consciousness. On a particularly
lucid morning, she asks, "When I'm dead, will you have more
daughters?"

"Of course not," says Meredith. "That's silly."

"If you do," says Celeste. "Tell someone old like Mr. Cohan.
That way, when he dies, he can tell me all about my new sister."

"Oh, darling," says Meredith. "I love you too much to have any
other children."

"Really?"

"I promise."

But Meredith doesn't like the thought that Arthur Cohan will
likely die sooner than she will, although this is biologically obvi-
ous. Sometimes, she catches him looking up at the house. Maybe
he is ashamed about the toxic root. Or—and she has learned to
be cynical about romance—maybe he is cleverly biding his time.
But to what end? The truth is, that if her daughter were healthy,
Meredith would be swooning over this man.

One evening, apropos of nothing, Maricel reveals that she has
no children. "When I was eight years old, all I wanted were babies,"
she says. "To play house with. To dress up in fancy silks. But I'm
too selfish to have children."

"You never know," says Meredith. "You seem like you'd make
a great mother."

"I make a great nurse. There's a difference," says the nurse. "Say, honey, that man's going to stare a hole through the window."

"What man?" asks Meredith.

Maricel says nothing.

"He just wants me to help him with his gardening. He's trying to restore the land to what it was like in Revolutionary times."

"Uh-huh," says the nurse. "If you say so."

"I do say so," answers Meredith.

"Fine by me. But when a man wants help gardening, he usually hires a gardener."

The nurse hums to herself in knowing amusement. This is too much to bear.

Meredith crosses to the bed and feels her daughter's forehead. She does this mechanically, even though the girl is not feverish. Just doped up and dying. She kisses her daughter's bony wrist. Then she heads down the back steps and onto the frost-hardened yard.

Three-quarters of a moon rests low in the late afternoon sky. A flock of songbirds are black outlines perched along the power lines. Cohan's face is blotchy and plastered with perspiration. He hands her the second shovel. "Most of this is kudzu," he says. "Some raspberries are mixed in—you can tell by the thorns—but I think they may have to be sacrificed. We can replant in the spring."

"Kudzu," she says. "It sounds like a Japanese curse."

"It is, in a way," says Cohan.

After that, they work side by side in silence. But Meredith is ever aware of her neighbor's presence, of his sturdy shoulders muscling through soil. She chops at the dead vines as best she can—and this does make her feel better. Or at least foggy. Cohan labors like a man paid by the weight of his crop. He clears fifty square yards in a matter of hours, driving his blade into the stony earth, undaunted by cold or wind. Meredith's entire body feels numb, but she doesn't dare complain. When the last of the sunlight fades over the crest of the hill, Cohan tosses his shovel into a mound of uprooted vines.

"I'm glad you came out here," he says.

He walks toward her and puts his arms around her waist. And this time he does kiss her—though, to her own surprise, she does not kiss back. She tries, but she keeps thinking of her daughter. She looks over Cohan's shoulder—at the dark square on the darker silhouette that is the window of Celeste's bedroom—and she breaks away.

· · · · ·

The house is still and silent and chilly when Meredith enters. It reminds her of the other empty houses that she once visited with realtors—always thinking of the future possibilities, not the previous owners and their losses. All of the downstairs lights have been turned off, and in the upstairs corridor, both bulbs have burned out. In her daughter's bedroom, the blinds are drawn shut. The nurse has dozed off in a rocking chair. Celeste has tucked the sheets under the mattress and folded the afghan into a perfect rectangle. Slow Poke, the girl's stuffed tortoise, sits alone atop the neatly layered bedding. Somehow, none of this surprises Meredith. She senses that the end is near—that her daughter is hiding in the clock. For the first time in months, she knows what she must do.

In the kitchen, she pours water into a pot and sets it on the gas range. Then she retrieves the toxic root from the pantry. Its pulp is deathly white. When she dunks it into the boiling water, it falls to the bottom with a thud. The liquid extract appears soapy. Meredith pours it into a cocktail glass. Like a fine liqueur.

Outside, Art Cohan stands at the far end of the lawn. He is still staring up at her house. Leaning on his shovel. He looks so solid, so invincible. The sort of man who would have made General Washington proud.

Meredith opens the clock cabinet and steps over the threshold, pulling the light oak doors shut behind her. It has been many years since she has been inside this compartment. At first, the ceiling seems low and tight. The aroma of damp wood is nearly overpowering. But gradually, her eyes adjust to the darkness.

She wades deeper into the belly of the clock. She passes though the widening corridors, increasingly bright, past Odysseus and Agamemnon and Helen of Troy. There is Darlene Cohan, swan-like, watering a geranium. And her own father, polishing his gold pocket watch. And Mama! Dear, dear Mama! Decked out to the nines on her way to the Chamber of Commerce dinner. They call out for her to stop, but she keeps going.

Celeste is only yards ahead of her, still carrying the toy talking clock. Meredith shouts out her daughter's name, and the girl turns around, surprised, like Orpheus caught off guard by Eurydice. She is wearing a long white gown. A pale jonquil is pinned into her intricately-coiffed hair.

"What are you doing, Mama?" she cries. *"You don't belong here."*

And the girl keeps protesting, but with increasingly less vigor, while Meredith hugs her in her arms and squeezes tight.

The Resurrection Bakeoff

Word came of the third resurrection while Amber's mother was serving tea. We were relaxing on Zelda's mahogany deck in Laurendale, soaking in the balmy spring morning and the scent of the blossoming peonies. My mother-in-law's kitchen radio was tuned to a Mozart Marathon—and the festive strains of the Haffner Serenade drifted through the open window. Then Virginia Public Radio broke into the recording to announce that a factory worker, recently decapitated by a metal press, had reappeared outside the gates of his Dayton, Ohio plant with his head intact. Zelda nodded knowingly, as though she'd foreseen this development all along.

"Well, doctor?" she said. "Riddle me that."

This I could not do. My wife's mother teaches folklore and comparative eschatology at the state university, and the previous week, after an oil rigger from Louisiana "woke up" at the morgue, Zelda was burning to anoint him a modern-day Lazarus. Sixteen years as a neurologist had rendered me somewhat more skeptical. *Death and taxes*, as they say. I was similarly doubtful when a teenager from Vermont disrupted her own funeral by pounding on the inside of her coffin lid. After all, we live in an age of hoaxes and swindles. Also, every profession boasts its share of incompetents, including medicine—and, even in this era of technological wonders, patients are sometimes pronounced dead prematurely. In contrast, as I reminded my mother-in-law, there were *no* reported resurrections in the scientific literature. *None.*

"*I* can't explain it," I replied. "But *someone* will. Soon enough. And when they do, a lot of people will be sadly disappointed."

My mother-in-law frowned. "You're so sure of yourself, aren't you?"

"I don't make the rules, Zelda. I just play by them."

"And hope? And imagination? How do they fit into your rules?"

We'd had this conversation many times before, of course, in various guises, but it had acquired a sharper urgency now that Amber's cancer had returned and Rust Belt laborers were rising from the dead. What Zelda Marcus really meant was: *Miracles do happen. If my daughter is going to die, so be it, as long as she comes back to us in better shape than before.* I could confirm the first part. After six years of remission, Amber's disease had crawled from her liver into her spine and lungs. She *was* going to die. I have nothing against hope, you understand. *False* hope is what I object to.

"It must be so hard for that poor man," observed Amber. "And for his family."

"What's that?" asked Zelda.

"Psychologically speaking, I mean," my wife explained. She worked as a crisis counselor for the county, although she was on extended leave. "Grief is designed to be a one-way process. Undoing it might prove highly traumatic."

"Not to mention the practical considerations," I added. "What if his children have already squandered their inheritance? Or if his wife is dating again?"

Zelda dried the base of her teacup with her paper napkin. "Well, it's a trauma that I could live with," she declared. "If Amber's daddy strolls through those doors tomorrow morning, you won't hear me complaining."

My wife's father drowned when she was eleven—and it struck me that Zelda's life had not changed much in the intervening three decades. She had no skeletons to hide, no replacement lover to conceal beneath her mattress. Nor did I suspect that Jack Marcus, a trusts-and-estates attorney of impeccable reputation, would have divulged any of the secrets that he'd previously carried to the grave.

"Trust me, Zelda," I said. "At the end of the day, this decapitated guy will turn out to have had a twin brother, or something like that."

"We'll see, doctor." Zelda only ever used the title *doctor* ironically. "Maybe there are more things in heaven and earth than are dreamt of in your philosophy."

As she so often does after claiming the final word, my mother-in-law conveniently excused herself to the restroom. That left me alone on the deck with my wife, the embers of death rekindled in the gentle spring air. On the great lap of lawn beyond Zelda's rose garden, the resident robins and starlings mingled with a flock of migratory geese. Behind the privet hedge, Zelda's neighbors tossed around a football. Sprinklers pulsed in the opposite yard. Virginia Public Radio had returned to the *menuetto galante* of the Haffner Serenade.

"I'm going to miss you and Mother arguing," said Amber. "I never thought I'd say that, but I really will."

She wouldn't miss anything, of course. Because she'd be dead. But we both understood exactly what she meant.

I circled behind Amber's chair and rested my palms on her frail shoulders. The bones were palpable beneath her flesh, like the frame inside a well-used sofa.

"Would you *want* to be resurrected?" I asked. "If it were possible..."

A long pause followed—so long, that I grew concerned Amber had lost the thread of the question, when she finally said, "I suppose it would depend how much time has gone by . . . and upon what *you* wanted. You and Mother . . ." She turned and pressed her tiny fingers to my lips. "Please don't say anything more, Charles. What you believe you want today, and what you will actually want, in years to come, are two very different things . . ."

So I said nothing. Because I knew she was right. As usual.

I was thinking about another woman, a folk musician named Rochelle Logan, whose resurrection I'd once longed for—and now feared more acutely than death itself.

. . . . .

My affair with Rochelle is not an episode that I am proud of, nor it is something that I can explain   not in any meaningful and satis factory way. The facts speak for themselves: Six years ago, shortly after her diagnosis, my wife started two months of experimental, in-patient chemotherapy at Methodist General in Petersburg, and in the course of visiting her, I struck up a liaison with a single mother who worked at the hospital gift shop. Deplorable, but true. My lover was one-quarter Cherokee with deep, tragic eyes and jet-black hair cascading to her waist. Rochelle had ambitions as a singer-songwriter, but they'd grown vague once she'd passed thirty. She was also a widow—her husband had succumbed to a glioblastoma on the same floor where my wife received her daily poison—and she listened well. I suppose that if Amber had died then, as was widely expected, I'd have married Rochelle Logan. Instead, the oncologists beat my wife's disease into remission, while Rochelle and her daughter asphyxiated in an electrical fire.

I pleaded with God for months to restore my lover. I bargained. I shouted. But I conducted all of my grieving privately. In public—

at Methodist General, on Zelda's porch—I was ever the devoted spouse. What never crossed my mind was owning up, or pleading for forgiveness, at least not until that teenager from Vermont revived during the 23rd Psalm and accused her uncle of strangling her. (Before that, the authorities had pinned the crime on a drifter who'd done odd jobs at her father's dairy farm.) The next morning, I heard on the news that an elderly Norfolk woman had admitted to poisoning her late husband, fearful that he might return from the grave for revenge. My thoughts drifted to my own gnawing secret. So when the factory worker in Ohio reemerged with his head on his shoulders, I was already far less confident in my skepticism than I'd made out to Zelda. By the time the first World War II vet materialized on the beachhead at Normandy, and that murdered prostitute incriminated those Reno councilmen, I was already contemplating a preemptive confession to Amber. Why wait for Rochelle Logan to appear upon our doorstep strumming her guitar?

I learned of the Nevada call girl's charges on the drive home from a racquetball match—not my regular Thursday night game, but a Tuesday evening stand-in for a surgeon who'd ruptured his Achilles' tendon—and I determined to unburden myself to Amber without delay. My wife was slaving away in the kitchen when I arrived home, as I'd expected, her forearms caked with flour, a dab of batter atop the bridge of her nose.

In January, she'd joined a support group, and the leader, a social worker who'd lost a leg to chondrosarcoma as a teenager, asked each participant to identify one goal that she hoped to meet before passing. Amber responded that she wanted to win the baking competition at our state fair. Honestly, if she'd announced a plan to take up mud-wrestling or cock-fighting, I couldn't have been more shocked. In our twenty years together, my wife's culinary endeavors had never extended beyond scrambling an egg or ordering a pizza. Now she revealed to me a distant memory of accompanying her paternal grandmother to the bakeoff, and how, for her, cobblers and tarts represented *the path not taken*, a yearning so secret that she'd suppressed its very existence since her adolescence. "Or it's a baby substitute," she'd said—offhandedly, though not casually enough to mask her regrets.

The next morning, Amber circled the final Sunday of September on her calendar and purchased enough non-stick bakeware to lodge a battalion of Pillsbury Doughboys. And I give her credit. Even as her appetite declined through the spring, she wouldn't let a day pass without a foray into rhubarb or banoffee or meringue.

Amber greeted me with a broad smile and a slice of pie. Our evening ritual. I loosened my necktie, set my attaché case on a kitchen chair and kissed the prow of her forehead. She pressed a fork into my hand, desperate for a verdict.

"Taste," she ordered.

One of the ironies of Amber's quest was that her cancer had killed not only her appetite, but also her taste buds. So she spent all day baking, then waited for my tongue to judge her output. Like a deaf Beethoven, asking his beloved Therese, *"Ist es nicht schön?"*

"Fantastic," I declared. "What is it?"

"Well, your favorites were the pineapple pecan and the strawberry coconut," Amber explained, beaming. "So I merged them. You're sampling a gastronomic first: pineapple-pecan-strawberry-coconut-buttermilk pie." She wiped her hands on her apron, clouding the air with flour, and drew up a chair beside mine. "So it's decided? That's my recipe?"

"I can already see the trophy on our mantelpiece."

Amber hugged my arm. I reached forward and gently wiped the batter from her face, then licked my fingers clean. The idea of a confession, which had seemed so promising on the expressway, now churned my guts uncomfortably.

"I heard there was another one today," I ventured. "In Nevada."

She already knew. "Do you think they're real?" she asked.

As real as anything else, I wanted to say—which meant, I had no idea. Rochelle Logan no longer seemed real to me. Our stolen moments together in the gift shop stockroom seemed as much a fantasy as a cure for cancer. "My mind says no," I answered, "but the evidence increasingly seems to shout yes."

"Mother called. Do you remember how, last weekend, you said that factory worker's wife might have started dating again...?"

"Vaguely."

"Well, *she* does. She's convinced herself that my father is going to show up for breakfast one of these days, and she's afraid he'll be displeased that she went out with some veterinarian from Newport News twenty-five years ago." Amber rose abruptly and carried the pie dish to the sink. "She was *genuinely* upset, Charles. They went out on something like *three* dates when I was in college—and now she's all worked up about whether or not she should tell my father. She's getting impossible." Amber sighed and turned on the faucet. "Have you heard anything about if the returnees know what happened while they were gone?"

I acknowledged that I hadn't. "But I'm sure your dad will forgive her."

"She is too," said Amber, over the running water. "That's not the issue. The question is whether or not he'd want to know about the dates."

"Would you?"

"I'd trust your judgment either way," she replied. "It's not like they were still married, after all. Father had been dead for *eight years*. How could he possibly expect her to plan her life around the remote possibility that he'd come back?"

Amber shut off the tap and dried her arms on a dishtowel. The fluorescent ceiling bulb limned her face a gloomy violet, and her fragile body looked nearly diaphanous—not strong enough to carry a secret. Outside, the neighbor's dachshund barked for its supper. I crossed the kitchen and wrapped my arms around my wife, but said nothing. I was willing to risk allowing her one more night of peace.

· · · · ·

One night drifted into a second, then a third. By the end of June, the authorities had confirmed two hundred seventy-four resurrections, while another thirty or so claims remained under investigation. In May, these incidents had bumped earthquakes and tornados from the headlines; now, the media reported them reluctantly, as a thankless and time-frittering duty, after the names of the war dead overseas. None of the countless government epidemiologists and freelance parapsychologists probing the phenomenon had made any headway in explaining who came back, or why, nor did demographic patterns emerge—except that the majority of the resurrected had been dead fewer than fifty years, with the most remote born only during the Fillmore Administration. Nor did there appear to be any reason why some returned as senior citizens, and others in the prime of life, or why one Kansas housewife, who'd died at eighty-seven, reappeared in her nine-year-old body. The resurrected, incidentally, had no clue what had happened while they'd been gone. As a dyed-in-the-wool Washington Senators fan told his local newspaper: "Last thing I remember, it was June 3, 1919, and Walter Johnson had a 2-0 count on the Brown's George Sisler—and then I had trouble breathing."

Here in central Virginia, the first returnee was Mabel Steinhoff, a German-born domestic who'd once worked for Amber's grand-aunt. Zelda insisted that we drive out to Hydesville to pay the old woman a visit.

We made the trip on a Sunday morning. My mother-in-law had phoned ahead to arrange the meeting with the resurrected woman's grandson—a seventy-two year-old ex-boxer—and we found the pair of them playing checkers on a splintered picnic table outside a mobile home. Mrs. Steinhoff, a rotund, chinless creature, who looked as though she'd passed the afterlife gorging on jelly donuts, smiled at us vacantly.

The grandson, Hiram Jenks, remembered my mother-in-law from grammar school—and the pair embraced like kissing cousins. Then he offered me a meaty handshake. Amber presented him with a freshly-baked raspberry cheesecake.

"Much obliged, ma'am," he said. "What a strange world, isn't it? Who ever thought I'd be playing checkers with my own Grandmama?"

My mother-in-law settled down alongside Mrs. Steinhoff.

"Mabel?" said my mother-in-law. "It's me. Zelda. Alice Larue's daughter."

"I'm afraid to say Grandmama's memory isn't what it ought to be," explained Jenks. "She had a couple of strokes before she passed, last time. When it comes to anything that happened before her return, she's pretty much hit or miss."

Zelda ignored this warning. She clasped the elderly domestic's hand between both of her own, and asked, "Have you seen Jackson Marcus?"

Mrs. Steinhoff blinked vigorously—as though waking from a nap. "I really couldn't say," she replied. "Hiram? Have we seen Jack's son?" Then she turned to my mother-in-law and inquired, "I'm sorry, but what did you say his son's name was?"

"Please, Mabel. *Think*. Not Jack's son. *Jackson*. Jackson Marcus. A tall, frightfully handsome man smoking a corncob pipe." Chords of desperation rose in Zelda's voice. "*Please* think. Did you run into him while you were gone?"

"Gone where?" asked Mrs. Steinhoff.

"When you were *dead*," snapped Zelda. "I want to know whether you crossed paths with my husband while you were dead."

"Please, Mother," interjected Amber.

"It's all right," said Jenks—who displayed the crooked nose and dashed teeth of a fighter, but angelic blue eyes fit for a choirboy. He lit a cigarette off a lighter shaped like a pistol. "If I were in your shoes, I'd be asking the same questions."

"Jackson Marcus," pressed Zelda. "He wears a tweed jacket with elbow patches."

My mother-in-law had been fixated on her late husband's return for weeks. She'd cleaned out her spare room, so that he'd have an office, and she'd taken to preparing his favorite meals, on the off chance that he arrived hungry. On Tuesday, she'd dragged Amber to the Gentleman's Depot in Hanover Crossing to pick out collared shirts. Zelda had as much confidence in her husband's eventual return as I did that the sun would rise in the east. Meanwhile, I had my own set of inquiries for the demented lady—questions that I dared not ask. Had she encountered a thirty-two year-old dimpled beauty who played "Blowing in the Wind" and "Lemon Tree" on a steel-string acoustic guitar? Did the musician have an olive-skinned toddler in tow? Could she tell me if this woman had found peace? Or was Rochelle biding her time, waiting to emerge from the hereafter and avenge herself ruthlessly upon my own happiness? Mabel Steinhoff couldn't answer these questions, of course. Her memory of the years since her departure was as blank as the expression on her plump, docile face.

I suddenly realized that my eyes were misting up, and I dabbed them with my handkerchief. Amber noticed too. She wrapped herself around my elbow. She thought I was crying because our time together loomed so short, not because I had used it so poorly. "I adore you," she whispered.

Although I'd seen more than enough of Mabel Steinhoff to know that I was ready to return home, Hiram Jenks asked us to join him for a glass of "homemade lemonade," and Zelda graciously accepted.

The beverage Jenks served tasted like a Tom Collins, but packed the punch of Kentucky bourbon. My mother-in-law polished off two glasses while listening to our host describe his grandfather's attempt at rabbit farming, and the bout he'd *almost* fought against Rocky Marciano, and myriad other irrelevancies. Every so often, Zelda broke off listening to ask Mabel if she'd recalled Amber's dad. By the time we departed Hydesville, thunderclouds had steamrolled over the afternoon sun.

"She's holding out on us," declared Zelda. "Maybe not *intentionally*. But somewhere in that addled mind of hers, she knows where Jack is."

"Would it matter?" I asked.

"Of course, it would matter," snapped my mother-in-law. "How can you even ask that? Any news is better than nothing."

I wasn't so sure. *What if Amber's father doesn't want to come back?* I couldn't help wondering. *What if the departed have a choice whether to return—and your dead husband and my dead mistress have both declined?* All I said was, "I'm sure if she does remember anything, Hiram Jenks will phone you."

We dropped Zelda off in Laurendale and then inched north on the interstate, surrounded by inbound traffic from the beaches and the Civil War battlefields. On the radio, CBS news was reporting that one of the original Ziegfeld Girls had shown up for work at the *Jardin de Paris*. I flipped to an Oldies station.

"Thank you," said Amber.

"For what?"

"For loving me so much."

I responded by reaching across the gearshift and squeezing her wrist. A moment later, we pulled up in front of our home in Culpepper Heights—and an olive-skinned toddler in a diaper came charging along the flagstone path toward our sedan. My soul went cold. Then the girl's mother called after her—our neighbor, a sharp-featured, heavyset Cuban attorney who looked *nothing* like Rochelle—and the child stumbled.

Amber sprang to the child's rescue, gently cradling the sobbing girl until her mother stepped in. I was reminded of the many times that I'd watched Rochelle kiss a scraped knee, or tape a Band-Aid over an imaginary wound, and of the great injustice that my Amber would never raise a daughter of her own.

· · · · ·

That week witnessed the first wave of mass resurrections. Now the numbers were too large to process, like corporate layoffs or deaths from Pacific typhoons. Many of the returnees had no surviving kin and had to be housed in school gymnasiums and FEMA trailers. Not a day passed without sightings of deceased celebrities. Although many of these reports ultimately proved false, the mere possibility of running into Elvis or John Lennon while running errands had sixty-year-old divorcees flashing cleavage at the laundromat and the post office. Widows across the county joined Zelda in preparing the favorite meals of their late husbands—a logistical challenge for those who had married more than once—and, with each passing day, more of these women found their efforts rewarded. At the same time, the returnees brought with them century-old grudges and long-buried resentments. In one case, a resurrected pharmacist discovered his wife *in flagrante delicto* with her second husband, who happened to be the pharmacist's younger brother, and stabbed his replacement with a fireplace poker.

I did not expect any physical violence if Rochelle returned—just emotional fireworks. Yet I realized that might prove enough to shatter Amber's tenacity for living. My every encounter with a returnee served as a reminder that my own days of tranquility were numbered. When my third grade teacher, whose funeral I'd attended, accosted me in the Quick-Mart to tell me how proud she was of my accomplishments, I knew that I had to act.

That evening was one of the warmest nights of the summer. I waited until Amber had gone upstairs to bed, then slipped on the patio in my bathrobe and wrote out an uncensored confession in longhand. I measured each phrase like a potentially lethal elixir before committing the words to paper. It felt as though I was composing a suicide note. Somewhere in the distant darkness, revelers ignited volleys of illicit firecrackers. Fruit bats swept low in the yard. Moths circled the patio lamps. As I recorded the details of my affair with Rochelle—making no effort to mitigate my responsibility—I found myself reviling my late mistress. Why had she chosen me, of all her gift-shop customers, to invite into the stockroom? What right had she to shower me in such affection at a time when all seemed so hopeless?

My thoughts drifted and my pen fell to the page. The shadow of the Angel of Death suddenly shook me from my reverie, a long black scythe in the night. Seconds later, I registered that it was Amber herself who had stepped silently into the beam of the lamps.

"You okay?" she asked.

"Not really," I answered honestly. "Are you?"

Amber shook her head. "Two valium didn't even help," she said. "You're going to laugh at me when I tell you what's keeping me awake."

"I'd never laugh at you."

She allowed her wraithlike body to sink into the chair beside me. I slid my elbow over my confession.

"Have you ever heard of Theodora Smafield?" she asked.

"Never," I replied. "Do I want to?"

"Theodora Smafield was the world's foremost pie-baker during the Golden Age of Pie Baking. When pies mattered," explained Amber. "She won the Pillsbury Bakeoff in 1949, the Great American Recipe Competition in 1950, and practically every blue ribbon awarded for piestry over the next two decades... and I heard on the radio this afternoon that she reappeared in her niece's kitchen last weekend and has been baking up a storm ever since." My wife took a deep, tremulous breath, and added, "Her niece lives in Richmond."

"And you're afraid she'll enter the state fair?"

"Of course, she will."

"Good," I declared. "That will make your victory all the sweeter."

Amber searched my face for conviction. "You really think I can beat her?"

"I'm sure of it," I said. "Your pies are like ambrosia. Anyway, she may not turn out to be all that she's cracked up to be. People had simpler tastes back then. Lower expectations."

This was precisely what Amber needed to hear. A gleam of delight spread upward from her smile to her sharp, deep-set eyes. "You always know exactly what to say," she said.

That was when I knew that I would *never* show her the confession. My best hope, from that moment forward, lay in Rochelle Logan's ongoing absence. Maybe she had reunited with her first husband in the hereafter and wanted no part of me. Or, if Rochelle did return, maybe I could persuade her to keep our secret—as I had done, tryst after tryst, during the months when we both thought Amber's death was imminent. I'll confess that a third option also flickered across my mind. Murder. Not that I would actually silence Rochelle in that way—although I'm sure one could rationalize the killing of a returnee—but, for the first time, I understood how a man could kill his mistress to protect his wife. I also despised myself for wishing ill on a generous young woman who had never shown me anything but kindness.

"You're worried about me, aren't you?" asked Amber. "You're thinking I might not even make it to September..."

"Don't talk like that," I said. "Human beings aren't statistics. Nobody can predict with any certainly whether you have five years or fifty years. Got it?"

"You're the doctor," agreed Amber. "And even if I only have five days, maybe I'll get lucky and come back again before the autumn."

My wife stood up, bracing herself against the table, and kissed the back of my head. Then she dragged her body across the patio to the kitchen door.

"Don't stay up too late, all right?" she warned—and she was gone.

I waited until I saw the lights switched on in our bedroom window, and then switched off again, before I ripped apart my letter. Then I offered my bargain to the Unknown: *Please don't let her come back while Amber is alive, and I'll never ask to return again either.* My sacrifice carried unanswered across the darkness.

· · · · ·

Three weeks later, my wife collapsed in the produce aisle at Gwench's. That's technically in the Petersburg catchment area, so the ambulance transported her to Methodist General—even though Jefferson & Madison is probably closer. By the time I arrived, nearly two hours later, she was moored to an IV in the intensive care unit. Her admitting diagnosis read: *altered mental status*. The underlying reality was that she'd had a seizure. Her cancer, after months encamped within her spine, had launched a stealth assault against her brain.

I hadn't been inside an ICU in several months. My neurology practice focuses on movement disorders—Parkinson's disease, multiple sclerosis—and I encourage my patients to pursue hospice care in their final days, so few end up on ventilators. I wasn't prepared for the degree to which a summer of resurrections had transformed end-of-life care, changes summed up in a maxim markered across the dry-erase board behind the nurses' station: "The sooner they're gone, the sooner they can come back."

Amber's hospitalization occurred at the height of the second great wave of reappearances, the "August Maximum" that followed the "Midsummer Minimum." For several weeks in late July, resurrections had slowed to a trickle. A pair of economists at M.I.T. had linked this decline to changes in the sunspot cycle. They predicted that resurrections would end entirely—"a return to the permanent mortality status quo"—by August 1st. Instead, after a brief lull, the number of returnees soared into the millions. This brought joy to an untold number of families and exacerbated the housing crisis. For those still waiting, like Zelda Marcus, every waking moment was charged with anticipation.

My wife sat propped on a bower of pillows. What amazed me was how strong Amber seemed for a woman with cancer cells nibbling through her gray matter. She looked frail, yes—but not as though she might soon cease existing. That was the nasty thing about brain metastases: they lulled you into unwarranted optimism.

"I thought I might run into you here," she said.

Her voice betrayed her condition: strained, distant, breathless.

"Next time you're going to collapse in the supermarket, can't you at least give me some warning?" I asked. "How about eighty years?"

"You wouldn't want me to be so predictable, would you?" she asked, forcing a smile. "You'd get tired of me rather quickly."

I locked my fingers around hers, relieved that my wife's personality appeared intact. That's not always the case with seizures in advanced cancer patients. Sometimes the humanity evaporates, leaving behind only a fleshy shell.

Amber laughed unexpectedly—a sharp, hoarse burst of laughter that at first I mistook for choking. "So Theodora Smafield is going to win her blue ribbon after all," she said. "All that baking suddenly seems so silly...so frivolous..."

"Don't think that way," I shot back. "To hell with Theodora Smafield."

We sat together for another hour, talking for the sake of hearing each other's voices, until the transport crew arrived to convey Amber to her MRI. As soon as she'd gone, a senior attending approached me: a tall, drooping spirit with a hangdog white mustache. He'd clearly been waiting for an opportunity to speak with me alone.

"Mr. Windham?" he asked.

"Dr. Windham," I answered, shaking his hand. "I'm a neurologist."

My revelation caught him off-guard and he paused to recalibrate. Then he introduced himself as Dr. Todd Sewell, the head of the critical care unit. "I'd let you view the CT-scan, but honestly, I'm not sure I'd want to see it," he explained. "I'm sorry."

"Me too," I answered.

"For what it's worth," said Sewell, "I had another case like this about a month ago...a woman in her early twenties with kidney mets everywhere...no prognosis, really...and the patient came back in under a month. At the beginning of that first wave of returnees. Now she's in school again, as happy as ever." The elderly physician patted my shoulder. "It's a different world these days, Dr. Windham. There's always hope."

Sewell filled me in on the results of Amber's lab tests. He sounded far more confident relating potassium levels and white blood cell counts than he did while speaking of the Unknown. I'm afraid that I'm the same way with my own patients. When Sewell excused himself with a second pat on my shoulder, I was grateful for his departure.

I hurried down the service stairs to the ground floor. They'd renovated the main lobby since my affair with Rochelle, so the gift shop now occupied a free-standing hexagonal kiosk opposite the cafeteria. Our treasured stockroom had been replaced by a public alcove packed with ATMs and vending machines. While grieving, six years is a long time. In hospital planning, six years is an eternity. But what better choice did I have? My departed mistress had been cremated, her ashes spread by plane over the Blue Ridge. The cluttered aisles of "Today's Treasures" offered the closest proximity to Rochelle that I could imagine in this lifetime.

I fell to my knees between the plush animals and the knit-goods, indifferent to the stares of the other customers, and I prayed. "Please, Rochelle. Don't come back..." I took a deep breath and added, "All I'm asking for is a few more weeks."

. . . . .

Amber's condition declined in fits and starts, like a ball bouncing down a corridor of ramps and stairs. Zelda and I spent our days at her bedside, trying to keep up her spirits. I no longer challenged by mother-in-law's prophesies of miraculous recovery, her predictions of bakeoff victories to come. But I knew Amber wasn't fooled. My wife merely smiled and nodded politely, as though humoring a child or a lunatic. By the end of the first week in the hospital, she could no longer raise her head off the bed. I was so immersed in her care—and in absorbing those precious, evaporating moments—that I lost track of events in the outside world. Days passed before I learned the dramatic news: The resurrections had stopped.

As with any pandemic, the realization did not occur suddenly. Word of resurrections continued to trickle in from remote locations—so it wasn't until mid-week that the media reported the abrupt cut-off. By the weekend, every television station in America was broadcasting snippets of an interview with a sharecropper's daughter, Ida Barnswallow, who claimed to be the very last of the returnees to return. Everybody wanted to know her secret, as though she'd lived to an unheard of age. "Dumb luck," she explained, aglow with recaptured youth. "Never opened a Bible after I got married and certainly never ate no yoghurt nor whatnot. Just minded my own damn business and tried to have as much fun as possible."

I discussed these developments with my mother-in-law while Amber dozed under the sway of exhaustion and morphine.

"So what now?" asked Zelda. "It all seems so hopeless."

"Maybe they'll start again," I offered. "We have no way of knowing."

Zelda sighed. "I can't help thinking that Jack *was* going to come back—that his return was part of the cosmic design—and that something happened, something unexpected, that threw the plans of the universe off course."

"It may still happen yet," I replied—wanting to believe.

I sat beside Amber through the remaining twilight, already missing my wife's love, but also reflecting upon Rochelle Logan and how much I had dreaded her resurrection. Slowly, incrementally, my fear was replaced by yearning: the desperate, helpless longing for the departed that overcomes us once we recognize that they will never return.

The Orchard

· · · · · · · · · · · · · · · · · · ·

Once my father was settled into the nursing home—or as settled as a fifty-year-old can be among octogenarians—my mother relinquished the trappings of Conservative Judaism and returned to her secular gentile roots. The process was gradual. She stopped lighting candles on Friday evenings, started paying bills on Saturday afternoons. Our diet came to include swordfish, then squid, and finally one weekend, for a meeting of her book club, she prepared open-faced cucumber sandwiches on white bread. The sandwiches were cut into thirds and garnished with peeled apple slices. My mother's newfound friends, mostly older women she'd met volunteering at the branch library, lamented the decline of the city: the Roseann Quinn murder, the demise of automats and *The Herald-Tribune*, the escalating price of tickets to first-run movies. My mother spent much of the day refilling teacups. After our company departed, in a flurry of cheek-kissing, she sat me down in our partially-refurbished kitchen—a project frozen in time like a clock on a sunken ocean liner—and asked what I would think of moving to Connecticut.

"Jeez. You've got to be kidding," I said. Feeling that was not enough, and being in the depths of the bleak T. S. Eliot period that preceded my fourteenth birthday, during which I served up

Prufrock and *The Wasteland* the way other boys serve up baseball statistics, I added:

> *Connecticut is the longest state, connecting*
> *New York and Rhode Island, mixing*
> *Zilch and nothing and nada . . .*

"Please," said my mother. "It could be nice."

"It's nice here," I said. This wasn't true—it hadn't been nice for us in a long time—but it sounded plausible. "What's in Connecticut?"

"A situation," said my mother.

She passed me the newspaper. She'd circled an advertisement in the classifieds, under the heading SITUATIONS AVAILABLE. It was the only listing under that heading, between HELP WANTED—FEMALE and SEASONAL. This particular "situation" was a "60+ widower w/granddaughter" in search of "housekeeping and discourse."

"How very *Great Expectations*," I said.

"It's in the country," said my mother. "I looked it up in the atlas."

"Bully for you. I *do not* want to move to Connecticut."

"Keep an open mind, honey. It could be fun . . . I'm sure there's a lake nearby where we can go swimming."

"Which part of 'I do not want to move to Connecticut' don't you understand? *I do not want to move to Connecticut.*"

"Well, I do," snapped my mother, who throughout my father's decline had remained self-possessed and stoic as a candlestick. "I feel like if I don't get out of here—this apartment, everything—I'm going to spontaneously combust." She held her hands extended in front of her face, like Moses carrying the two tablets, as though examining her empty palms might yield great wisdom. Her bare, bony arms trembled. "I don't owe it to anybody to go through life unhappy. Not your father, not you—not anybody."

My mother stopped speaking and walked to the window. I picked up the salt shaker and inspected it closely, then trailed salt granules across the Formica tabletop like lines of cocaine.

"You know I'm on the verge of tears all day," said my mother. "I keep telling people it's an allergy—like goldenrod or God-knows-what—but what it really is is misery. *Misery.*"

"Why are you telling me this?" I said. "I'm your son. You're not supposed to tell me these things."

"Don't you think I know that?"

. . . . .

The man in search of "housekeeping and discourse" was inauspiciously named Grover Gallows, but he went by the nickname "Happy." Happy Gallows was indeed past sixty, possibly past seventy, but tall and robust. He wore a Breton mariners cap embroidered with an anchor badge. He smoked cigars. His fiefdom was a colonial farmhouse with Dutch doors and a sprawling adjacent orchard, where the public paid to harvest apples and strawberries and quinces.

"This older wing dates from the 1740s," said Gallows, giving us the realtor's tour. He'd already fed us apples out of the burlap sack hanging beside his waist, an offering far more Santa Claus than serpentine. "The newer wing—that's where your rooms will be—if we should decide we're a good fit, that is—came along circa 1790. They say Washington slept here, but more likely he stopped in for a pint of ale on the way through to Waterbury."

We passed under low-cut doorways and beneath exposed oak rafters. The rooms were pleasantly cool and smelled of fresh timber; the furniture was a smorgasbord of period pieces, but from different periods. In the den, a bearskin rug lay in front of the large-screen television.

"How long has this place been in your family?" asked my mother.

"It hasn't," answered Gallows. "I bought it nine years ago. Before that, I used to trade currency."

"Really?" answered my mother, surprised.

"You were hoping for good old Yankee stock, weren't you? Sorry to disappoint." He smiled through his thick gray beard. "We might as well get this out of the way at the outset. I'm a Mormon. Latter Day Saints. But a very lax one, at that. What they call a jack-Mormon. My late wife was the real deal. She grew up with it."

"A jack-Mormon," echoed my mother—trying the phrase on like a coat.

"Like a jackrabbit. Good at running away from things."

My mother looked quizzically at Gallows. He chuckled.

"A joke, Mrs. Flieger—the part about the rabbits."

"I wasn't sure."

"If—before I got married—you'd told me that a woman could make a Mormon out of me, I swear I'd have laughed my pants off. Then I met Dotty... The truth is that I used to be a Jehovah's Witness. When I was a kid. I thought it was awful—no birthdays, no Christmas. My Aunt—Sister Bernice Mathilda—made us preach door-to-door on Halloween every year as a test of our moral fortitude..."

"That's just awful," said my mother.

"It was what it was. It's easy to complain about the holes in your shoes until you see a man without feet... But, as I was saying, that's one of the reasons I chose this place... There was a *pogrom* near here right after Pearl Harbor. Because a handful of Witness children wouldn't salute the flag during parade drill. The locals burned down the Kingdom Hall, tarred-and-feathered the presiding overseer, and lynched two farmhands from that basswood opposite the old carriage house."

"Good Heavens."

"It turns out the farmhands weren't even Witnesses. Just deaf-mutes ... They don't teach you about that in school, do they, Josh?"

I shrugged. "In eighth grade we did world history."

Gallows' eyes glowed. "I hope you studied the Greeks. Pericles. Solon. The cradle of civilization."

"Kind of," I said.

"When I retired," continued Gallows, now addressing my mother, "I'd always planned to go back and study the Ancients."

"I'm afraid I don't know much about Ancient Greece," said my mother. "I read some Shakespeare in college. That's about it."

"Where there's a will, there's a way," said Gallows. "And often a codicil, I might add ... But I was getting to the important part. My daughter died nine years ago. And my son-in-law. In a freak ballooning accident."

"I'm sorry," said my mother.

"A lightning bolt cut lose the passenger basket," added Gallows, making a ski-slope motion with his hands to mimic the course of the attack. " ... That's when Dotty and I moved up here with Oleana."

Our host walked to an end table and retrieved a snapshot of a teenage girl that had been tucked into the frame of another photograph. She was stunning: deep-set black eyes, flawless skin, a brow arched to classical proportions. It was the dead daughter, I realized, not the living granddaughter.

"She was beautiful," said my mother

I agreed quickly, handing the photo back to our host. I was afraid that if I held it too long, I might damage it—like a precious rock formation sensitive to human touch.

"And you, Mrs. Flieger ... You're divorced?"

"My husband's dead."

My mother had warned me to expect this—that a small lie would make everything easier—but as much as I despised my father, his "death" was a big stone to swallow.

Gallows looked my mother over and nodded. "Don't take this the wrong way, Mrs. Flieger, but I'm very glad you're a widow."

. . . . .

Happy Gallows' enterprise, McLaughlin's Farms, occupied twenty-eight acres of rolling terrain between County Route 17 and the Taukatuck River. The apple trees represented successive expansions of the orchard—McIntoshes and Cortlands planted in the 1950s, Macouns and Empires from the early 1970s, a hodge-podge of Pippins and Jonagolds and Spartans that Gallows had put in during his own first years on the land. There were thirty-six cultivars all told, as well as three varieties of pears. Another couple fields were devoted to additional crops: berries, gourds, pumpkins, yellow sweet corn and Indian corn. The remaining acreage had been sown with Sudan grass in preparation for apple seedlings. Gallows called this fallow lot the "church field"—as distinguished from the "main field"—though there didn't appear to be any evidence of a church. Since two months remained before the start of the school year, our new landlord set me to work plowing "green manure" into the soil. I also laid down tamarisk windbreaks and repaired stone walls. Gallows paid me the same rate he paid the college students who sat behind the long wooden check-out tables in the parking lot and weighed the customers' fruit. On weekday afternoons, when business was light, he hiked out to assess my progress. Also to share with me his knowledge of apples.

"The history of civilization is the history of apples," was one of Gallows' favorite expressions, and he had a trove of factoids to prove it. Did I know that the word "paradise" came from the Persian *pairidaeza*, appropriated by Xenophon to describe walled gardens of fruit? Or that St. Jerome had encouraged his monks to graft apples to escape from sloth and the devil?

I did not. I missed the takeout chop suey from Four Brothers, and riding between subway cars over the Manhattan Bridge, and the book selection at the branch library on 78th Street. (The Westbury library, which was housed in a basement annex of the municipal building, was open only two mornings each week. It had children's books and local historic documents. Not much else.) I did not relate any of this to my employer.

Some mild afternoons, Gallows lured my mother away from her cooking and housekeeping, driving her down to my worksite in his pickup truck. Then he'd lay out a quintessentially New England lunch spread on a picnic blanket. Smoked ham. Cranberry sauce. Red wine in plastic glasses. He often wore a necktie on these outings.

"I've been teaching your son about the fruit tree business," Gallows said. "I think we'll make another Johnny Appleseed of him yet."

He retrieved an Ida Red from his satchel and polished it on his shirt.

"I want to be a poet," I said.

"You'd be surprised how many poems there are about apples," answered Gallows. "Milton. Columella. Not to mention *De Vegetabilibus* by Albertus Magnus of Cologne. His great quandary was whether fruit trees had souls."

"What an idea," said my mother.

"That's nothing, Lynn. Edward Bunyard called the crunch of apple-eating the sixth sense..."

My mother smiled. "Where do you come up with this stuff?"

"Now you see why I'm such a bad Mormon. I should be pondering the King Follett Discourse and the Articles of Faith—and instead I'm wondering whether apple trees go to heaven."

"I want to be a *real* poet," I said, more forcefully.

"He's a regular Robert Frost," offered my mother. She'd meant this as a compliment. (If I'd been a girl, I'd have been a regular Emily Dickinson.)

Gallows mopped his brow and rose to his feet. He coughed several times before declaiming:

> *My long two-pointed ladder's sticking through a tree*
> *Toward heaven still,*
> *And there's a barrel that I didn't fill*
> *Beside it, and there may be two or three*
> *Apples I didn't pick upon some bough.*
> *But I am done with apple-picking now ...*

"Bravo!" cried my mother, clapping her hands together.

"Not half-bad for an old man," countered Gallows. "You asked for Robert Frost, didn't you?"

I tied knots in the crabgrass, feeling the heat rise in my head. Against my better judgment, I muttered:

> *I grow old ... I grow old ...*
> *I shall wear the bottoms of my trousers rolled ...*

"Joshua," my mother said sharply.

"It's alright, Lynn," said Gallows. Then to me:

> *Shall I part my hair behind?*
> *Do I dare to eat a peach?*

"I admire a young man who knows his Eliot," he added. "And I particularly admire that part about the peach."

I could think of no reply to this, so I said nothing.

"We might yet marry off this poet of yours," said Gallows— with a directness utterly alien to my experience.

"Do you have anyone particular in mind, Hap?"

"I just might," he answered. "And she just might be coming home on Friday."

Gallows laughed so hard he nearly choked to death on his apple. He coughed a small piece of fruit into a handkerchief and started laughing again.

. . . . .

I had been contemplating my romantic prospects with Oleana long before her grandfather alluded to them. I was a fourteen-year-old boy, after all, and there weren't many fourteen-year-old girls hanging around our farmhouse. Only the weekend customers, sometimes, but they came with their parents—and the college guys who drove the farm wagons had first crack at them. In any case, I'd never managed to ask out any of the girls I'd gone to school with in New York City, so it didn't seem realistic that I'd succeed with a stranger on an outing with her family. But Oleana was another matter. She'd be living with us, after all. And I'd seen her photo in Gallows' study.

Oleana was away at summer camp in the Berkshires. At breakfast on Friday, butter pancakes with fresh blackberries, I made a conscious point of appearing utterly indifferent toward her arrival. When I got to the church field, I was so edgy with anticipation that I accidentally plowed through an irrigation hose. I got down from the tractor every half hour to urinate in the hedges. On one of these expeditions, Oleana surprised me from behind.

"Hey," she said. "I'm Oleana."

I nearly castrated myself with my zipper. "What are you doing here?"

Oleana grinned. "That's some welcome."

"I just thought . . ."

"Though *what*? That I'd sit on my ass all day waiting for you to come home? Grandpa wrote me all about you—about how you like dark poetry. He thinks we're going to be the best of friends."

I shoved my hands in my pockets and turned crimson.

"Are we going to be the best of friends?" she asked.

I could feel the fever reach the tips of my ears. "I guess so," I said.

"I'm sorry if I interrupted you..." Oleana continued. "I can come back when you're finished."

I wasn't certain whether she meant pissing or plowing. "No, I'm done."

"You sure? I don't want you wetting your pants on my account."

None of the girls I knew talked like that. "I'm sure," I said.

"Suit yourself."

We stood face to face through what seemed like a long silence, although it probably lasted only a few seconds. Oleana toyed with the metal snaps on her overalls, drawing attention to her upper-body development. I now suspect this was a calculated trick, passed down through generations of well-endowed country girls. I quickly lowered my eyes to her bead-tasseled moccasins.

"I should probably get back to work," I said, taking a couple of half-hearted steps toward the vacant field.

"Aren't you going to ask me anything?" she demanded.

"Like what?"

"I don't know. Like: how was camp?"

"How was camp?" I asked.

"Awesome," she said. "But that's probably because all I have to compare it with is Mormon camp." She explained how, in prior years, Mrs. Gallows—Grandma Dorothy—had insisted on her attending an LDS camp in Maine; she talked as though we'd known each other for decades. "Mormon camp was perfectly okay, but boring," said Oleana. "Lots of archery and badminton and lanyard weaving. You know—practical life-skills. But no smoking. No guys...Next year, I'm going on a teen tour."

Oleana perched herself on the tractor wheel. A dry leaf hung suspended in her long dark hair. Overhead, a solitary hawk swept toward the horizon.

"You know what?" said Oleana. "If we're going to be the best of friends, you should tell me a secret. Something nobody else knows."

"I don't know any secrets like that," I said.

Strictly speaking, this was the truth. After all, my mother also knew about how my father had been "caught" with a student—a *male* student, one of *many male students*—and how he had tried to blame these "interludes" on his multiple sclerosis medication. But my mother was right: it was far easier to have a dead father than a half-blind, demented one who'd been dismissed from a college teaching job on a morals charge.

"C'mon," pleaded Oleana. "Just for fun. Don't you trust me?"

"I *said*: I don't know any secrets . . . Let's talk about something else."

My companion frowned and nibbled her own hair, but her consternation was short-lived. "Here's what we'll do," she said. "I'll tell you a secret and *then* you'll tell me a secret. Okay?"

"I don't like secrets."

"Don't be a jerk," said Oleana. "You'll like my secret. It's really dark."

She launched herself off the tractor and darted across the high grass. I followed. We scattered entire villages of meadowlarks and field mice. Oleana glanced over her shoulder several times to make sure I was keeping pace. Her breasts jounced against the bib of her overalls. When we reached the hickory copse at the far edge of the church field, I collapsed in the shade. My side had cramped up. I could hardly breathe. I closed my eyes and sank into the cool bank of clover.

"Look at this," insisted Oleana.

I opened my eyes reluctantly. Oleana was holding a small amber bowl.

"You know what this is?" she asked.

"A bowl."

"A skull. A human skull."

"Shit," I said.

"There's tons of them out here. Under the field. There used to be a church for escaped slaves somewhere down by the river—and this field was their cemetery. One of the college guys who worked here last summer showed me how to dig for bones. We tried building a whole skeleton, but we were missing the fingers and toes."

My companion retrieved a spade from behind a large boulder. She dug out of the soil what looked like a turquoise woman's hatbox. The battered container held an assortment of human remains.

"We kept only the best specimens," explained Oleana. "At first, we saved basically everything we could get our hands on. Even bone chips and teeth. But by the end, we were much more selective . . . It's sort of like when you go on vacation to the beach. That first day you collect any seashells you can find, even broken ones, but the more you have, the higher your standards get."

I picked up one of the bones—probably a forearm. It was lighter than I expected.

"Does your grandfather know about this?"

"Don't you dare tell him," ordered Oleana. "It's a secret."

"But your grandfather's going to plant apple trees here—"

"*It's a secret*," repeated Oleana. "Just between you and me."

And the college guy who'd told her, I thought—but didn't say so.

"Okay," I agreed. "It's a secret."

Oleana lunged toward me and toppled me into the grass. She started kissing me, almost violently, although I was totally unprepared to be kissed—in fact, I had grass caught in my mouth. But I wasn't complaining. Then she broke off suddenly, so suddenly that I feared I'd done something wrong.

"If you tell anyone," she said, "I won't kiss you ever again."

After that, you couldn't have tortured the information out of me.

. . . . .

That was the first of many trips to the hickory copse. It was a small wooded peninsula between our fields and the neighboring horse farm. In the twilight, we could hear the college boys next door rounding up the horses—and once, we even heard a series of gunshots. I said they were probably shooting an injured animal, but Oleana insisted it was just target practice. "You don't unload a whole clip on one horse," she said.

"I guess not."

"I think it's cruel to shoot sick horses like that anyway," she added. "It's really barbaric. You wouldn't shoot an old woman if she broke her leg."

"Horses aren't people."

"Whatever," she said. "The two worst things in the world, as far as I'm concerned, are sharing secrets and hurting animals. And lying to your friends, of course."

Then she asked me, as she often did, about my father.

I tried to keep my falsehoods as focused as possible, but like many children who worship their parents—and Oleana gushed about Grandpa Happy on the slightest pretext—it was inconceivable to her that anyone might feel otherwise. She wanted me to miss my father the way she missed her Grandma Dorothy. Unfortunately, even before his downfall, my father and I had never been close. To his students at NYU—particularly the actively Jewish ones—he was like a parent: they sang Hebrew songs together after our *shabbus* dinners, prayed in the makeshift *sukkah* that he erected on the roof of our brownstone. In contrast, I always sensed that he viewed me as an afterthought, a concession—even as an impediment to his campus popularity. Not that he was anything but generous toward me, often too generous, but always in a distant and uninterested way. You might say I respected him, rather than loved him, so when that respect evaporated, there was nothing left. I still cannot imagine why my mother married him. I asked her once, right after the scandal, and she said he'd been different once. Less rigid. Besides, what coed didn't get a kick out of running off with one of her professors? That was all she could muster. So in my lies to Oleana, I did the man only kindness.

The difficult part was coordinating my fabrications with my mother in order to make certain that our stories gelled. But when I brought this up to her, one August afternoon when we went shopping for sneakers in Waterbury, she glared daggers at me. "Say anything you darn please," she said, clutching her purse to her chest like a teddy bear. When I tried to push the matter further, she removed a lone white cross trainer from the opposite shelf and asked what I thought of it. As a result, I had no choice but to spin my tales in the dark. Most of my offenses were sins of omissions: the disciplinary hearing, the pending divorce. Luckily, Oleana wanted to talk about her own grandmother, whom she could have eulogized continuously. My father was merely a foil—a source for solidarity.

(In contrast, Happy Gallows talked little of his late wife and much of my father. "A professor," he said. "If I could do it over again, I'd have been a professor." He liked to call me "the scholar" and declare, "The apple won't fall far from the tree." Another of his diversions was to tap me on the head with an apple and to declare me "our own Isaac Newton," though I felt more like the son of William Tell.)

Oleana's principal interest was mortality. She argued with herself over whether there was an afterlife—what she called a kingdom of eternal glory—or whether life was a one-shot deal. If there were a Celestial Kingdom for believers, she feared her grandfather might not be admitted. That he and Grandma Dorothy might be separated forever.

When we weren't talking about death, Oleana and I spent most of our time with our tongues in each other's mouths. We kissed in every position known to mankind—around the shoulder, rubbing noses like Eskimos, even waist-deep in the river. But we only kissed. The school year started. I was paroled from my orchard duties. Yet we continued our romantic forays into the copse. And *still* we only kissed. Then one day, I dared to slide my hand under Oleana's shirt.

"C'mon, Josh. Don't."

I drew back quickly. "Why not?"

"You know why not."

I *didn't* know why not.

"I'm sorry," I said. "I thought you might want a boyfriend."

Oleana straightened out her clothes. "You can't be my boyfriend," she said with frustration. "You're practically my brother."

"What's that supposed to mean? You don't think...?"

"Like, wake up. What planet do you live on?"

She was right, I realized. I got up and dusted off my jeans. I must have appeared very unhappy, because Oleana squeezed my wrist.

"We can keep kissing," she said. "Kissing is different."

. . . . .

How Happy Gallows went from being my mother's employer to my mother's suitor still remains something of a mystery to me. I suspect that form may have preceded function—that two single, lonely people eating month after month at the same dinner table are bound to ask themselves what might come next. But who knows? All I can say is that once my eyes were opened, I didn't see how things could have been otherwise.

At some point, my mother moved from the new wing to the old one. She came down to breakfast wearing one of Gallows' silk shirts.

Oleana's grandfather often went away on "apple business" for several weeks at a time—to inspect cultivars in the Catskills, in Rhode Island—and he returned with increasingly lavish gifts. Black truffles. A white gold necklace. Packages he warned my mother to open in private. He also made changes in his own life, including taking on a strict diet. His goal was to lose thirty pounds. "Better hungry than dead of a heart attack," he declared, gnawing on a carrot. In his zeal, he overshot his target; by Thanksgiving, my mother was working to put weight back on him.

"You're trying to fatten me up for market, that's what you're doing," he said. That same week, he grew vain about his bald spot, insisting my mother shave both his head and his beard. "Better to look like a convict than an old man."

They invited the Ukrainian couple who owned the horse farm over to dinner. Gallows told good-natured Mormon jokes ("Why can't you take one Mormon fishing? He'll drink all your beer."); he admitted that he grew tearful when he thought about windfall apples ("There's something profoundly sad about them. All that loss."); he sang a mildly indecent ballad recounting the adventures of twin fishmongers and a pair of prostitutes ("It's amazing what you pick up in the coastguard.") After each stanza, he churned up smoke from his thick cigar. My mother laughed—uncharacteristically—and demanded an encore.

Yet for all his *joie de vivre*, I think Happy Gallows' bond with my mother was sealed with parallel regrets. These rose to the surface only once, on the walk back from the unveiling of Dorothy's tombstone.

"I traded currency for thirty-eight years," he said. "Imagine that. And I never once thought how strange—how arbitrary—currency is. Billions of people all over the world agreeing that certain random pieces of paper are worth so much food or so much medicine.

But what's even more amazing is that I earned my bread guessing what other people thought those random pieces of paper would be worth."

My mother wrapped her elbow around his. "I never thought of it that way."

"It's not worth thinking about," said Gallows. "I don't know why I did it."

"Like not mixing meat with milk," said my mother. "All those years I used two separate sets of dishes—one for meat and one for dairy—and I have no idea why."

Gallows lit a cigar and tossed the match into the lane. "That's why I prefer to focus on the present. If you have one good day, nobody can take that away from you."

All in all, I decided Gallows would make a passable surrogate dad. I wanted to share my feelings with Oleana, to ask her if she thought her grandfather might propose to my mother, but she'd stopped taking me down to the hickory copse. In fact, she stopped spending much time with me at all. Or no more time than four-teen-year-old girls normally spend with their future stepbrothers (though we'd technically be step-siblings-once-removed, if her grandfather married my mother). Once, I walked down to the copse on my own and discovered an empty pack of cigarette butts and a torn, waterlogged pair of men's underpants. I didn't go near the church field after that.

We were already in the dead of winter when I finally built up the courage to ask my mother directly about her relationship with Gallows. The branches of the fruit trees had been wrapped with aluminum foil to protect them from blistering and sunscald. Long icicles hung off the eaves and drainpipes of the farmhouse. My mother had taken to strewing birdseed on the back patio and then painting the chickadees and juncos in watercolors, a hobby that suited her far more than hosting a book club. Gallows was away on one of his trips. Oleana and some older boys had gone across the river to sleigh on the slopes of Pilgrim's Hill. I sat down opposite my mother's easel and watched her delicate brushstrokes.

"I'm getting better, honey, don't you think?" she asked. "Soon I'll be like that fellow on PBS. The one who does a whole painting in an hour."

"Sure, Mom," I answered. "Can I ask you something?"

"I don't like the sound of that."

"Are you going to marry Oleana's grandfather?"

My mother stepped back, arms akimbo. "Why shouldn't I?"

"Chill out. I was just asking. No need to get so defensive."

"I'm sorry," my mother answered. She wiped her hands on her smock and sat down opposite me. "I don't know. He's *seventy-two* years old, Josh. *Seventy-two*. But these days a man in his shape can live to ninety-five. So who's to scoff at another twenty-three good years? Or even five?" She massaged her knuckles between her fingertips, trying to work out the arthritis. "I thought you liked him."

"I do like him," I said.

"Good," she said. "I do too."

I was going to inquire about the status of the divorce. Instead, I asked: "Why don't we ever visit my father?"

My mother twisted her lips to the side, a subtle sign of contempt. Other than that, she appeared shockingly unfazed. "He wouldn't know you were there," she said.

"*But still . . .*" I insisted.

"Do you *want* to visit your father?"

I walked to the china cabinet and toyed with one of the figurines. A tiny porcelain duck wearing a bonnet.

"I guess not," I said. And I didn't.

. . . . .

That might have ended matters there, at least for the time being, but something inside me wouldn't leave well enough alone. I suppose I was angry at Oleana for having a grandfather who was everything that my own father wasn't. And she *had* shattered my heart. That too. Adolescent heartbreak shouldn't be underestimated. The prospect of catching Oleana's grandfather engaged in some shameful indecency—as absurd as that now sounds—struck me at the time as the optimal revenge.

I had a second reason for my suspicions. My mother had recently asked Gallows if she might accompany him on one of his apple-hunting journeys—to southeastern New Jersey, where her college roommate worked as an elementary school nurse—and, without warning, he'd flown her to Capri for the weekend instead. She was delighted. I was too much my father's son not to find this incriminating.

They returned from Italy after Easter. Gallows rapidly scheduled a second trip. This time not to New Jersey, but across the burnt over country of upstate New York. Batavia. Geneseo. He was searching for Freyburg hybrids resistant to scabbing and powdery mildew, and he planned to be away longer than usual. Two weeks, maybe three. He'd save eight cents, he joked, by delivering the postcard to us himself.

Gallows departed before dawn, to avoid traffic. When his pickup pulled out of the gravel drive and onto the county highway, I was carefully concealed in the truck bed—beneath a polyethylene tarpaulin and surrounded by mossy wooden rails left over from the previous autumn's fencing.

My heart raced like a runaway's, but my skepticism quickly paid off.

We drove not west, but east, toward Waterbury. The signs for McLaughlin's marked our retreat: ORCHARD, NEXT LEFT; PIES AND PRESERVES, YEAR ROUND; PICK YOUR OWN APPLES, 1½ MILES. With the dawn came a steady cold rain. It tapped persistently on the tarpaulin. Fog filled the dips in the road; deer grazed on the embankments. The only human form we encountered for miles was a drooping scarecrow that had fallen from his perch. The straw man rested slumped on his knees, like a crime-victim pleading for mercy.

On the far side of the reservoir, the open country gave way to turn-of-the-century Victorian homes. Flags hung on many doors, also ornamental wreaths left over from Christmas. We worked our way toward the central business district, inching along behind a box-truck delivering the early morning edition of the *Republican-Advocate*. My mind wandered to Eliot's

> *Certain half-deserted streets,*
> *The muttering retreats*
> *Of restless nights in one-night cheap hotels . . .*

As though on cue, Gallows eased the car to the curbside opposite the Waterbury Holiday Inn. He carried his two valises into the office. I watched through the lobby window as he exchanged greetings with the desk clerk and handed over luggage for safekeeping. Then he flipped open his pocket-watch and exited.

Gallows walked briskly up Elm Street—past the state courthouse, the boarded-up shoe factory, the public fountains that had gone dry for the winter. I followed. We crossed the park commemorating the city's Civil War dead, where a banner suspended between to tent-posts proclaimed: WATERBURY, THE BRASS CITY and beneath that asked: "What Is More Lasting Than Brass?" Opposite the Methodist hospital, Gallows took one final puff of his cigar and descended to a basement door.

· · · · ·

I hitchhiked home that afternoon. The man who drove me was a Florida fish-and-game inspector collecting disability for a kidney problem. He'd come to visit his married sister in Waterbury, which, he informed me, was the city where the Mad Bomber had been arrested. "His real name wasn't the Mad Bomber," the man explained. "It was George something." When he dropped me off at the orchard parking lot, the lights were already lit inside the farmhouse.

Several unfamiliar cars sat parked at the top of the drive, including a state police cruiser. The kitchen door stood open. I waited until Oleana came down the back steps and headed out to the hickory copse for her smoke break.

"Where have you been all day?" she demanded. "You know your mother called the police. She thinks you were kidnapped by pirates or something."

She offered me a cigarette. I shook my head. The refuge where we'd kissed for so long was now littered with crushed soda cans.

"I followed your grandfather today," I said. "I hid in his truck."

Oleana frowned. "You shouldn't have done that."

I took a deep breath. "He didn't go to New York," I said. "He went to the doctor. A cancer doctor."

Oleana tossed her cigarette into a pile of leaves. It smoldered.

"I know that," she said.

"I don't understand."

"There's not much to understand," she said. "He has cancer. Of the throat."

"Does my mother know?"

"Of course, not. That would ruin things . . . What do you think all the head-shaving and dieting is about?"

I cupped an overhanging branch with my palms and let my body sway. "I don't get it. Your grandfather's going to die and he's keeping it a secret?"

"He's not going to die," she said sharply. "Some people make a full recovery." Oleana's tone softened. "He was diagnosed right after you came. But he's so happy now—with your mother...Sometimes I think he's even happier than he was with Grandma Dorothy."

"But he doesn't trust her enough to tell her the truth?"

"She's already lost one husband...If she knew he was so sick, she might not marry him. Or that's what he thinks, at least."

Deep down, I knew Gallows was right about this.

"He's going to propose when he gets back," she added. "He wants them to go through with it immediately."

"So he's going to try to dupe my mother into marrying him."

"Promise you won't tell her," said Oleana.

"That's impossible," I said—thinking of the interminable divorce proceedings. Not that that mattered.

"Please, don't say anything," pleaded Oleana. "I'm sorry I've been such a jerk...Really, I am. I just didn't think it was right to keep coming down here with you. Under the circumstances."

"I guess not."

"What else was I supposed to do?"

"I don't know," I said. "Something else, I guess."

She apologized again, but already I wasn't listening. I walked back up toward the farmhouse—slowly, but confidently. It was drizzling again. The ground in the church field was still hard from the frost. Then, as I crossed the orchard, the earth turned softer, and my feet sunk into the tragic mire of crushed windfall fruit.

The Grand Concourse

To celebrate her sixtieth birthday—she is now older than her parents when they died—my mother asks to take a daytrip. She has okayed it with the shrinks, she says. Dr. Fradkin agrees a twelve-hour pass will do her good. "His first name's Monty. Monty Fradkin. He's quite a good looking young man," says my mother. "If you were to ask me, I'd say he'd make a wonderful father for the baby."

"Does Dr. Fradkin know where you want to take you?" I ask.

"I'd snap him up myself, Lydia—only they have rules against that. So the headshrinkers don't take advantage of us, even if we *want* to be taken advantage of. One man's professional boundaries are another woman's enforced celibacy. Did you ever hear such nonsense? I'm suicidal, not syphilitic."

"I asked you a question, Mom. Does the doctor know where you want to go?"

"He's an open-minded man," says my mother. "If he *did* know, he'd approve."

We're sitting on one of the cast iron benches that line the footpath between Red Brick Cottage II and Red Brick Cottage III. Abington Manor feels more like a university campus than a psychiatric facility: waves of jonquils rising through beds of red woodchips, a Gothic revival chapel where the bells peal on the hour. Ten weeks have passed since my mother tried to drown her-self—long enough for the ice sheath to melt off Long Island Sound. The firemen who rescued her are now battling brushfires along the interstate. Jay Bergman, the veterinary student responsible for my positive pregnancy test, is dating a city planner. My mother has already worked her way up to "level three privileges," meaning she may explore the grounds without supervision. The tranquility is killing her slowly.

"Trust me, darling," she insists. "This is important. Some-day I won't be around anymore and *then* you'll have all sorts of questions. What will you tell the baby when she asks about her great-grandparents?"

"Babies don't ask questions," I say. "They can't talk."

My quip takes my mother by surprise. She's the clever one, the scalpel-tongued theater critic who dismisses two-hour Broadway productions with mordant, single-word reviews. I'm just a yoga instructor. While she plays dramatic executioner on the morn-ing talk shows, I adjust big-boned women into the lotus position. Don't get me wrong: I enjoy what I do. Unlike most of my friends, I haven't yet reached that point where I'm counting on my chil-dren to make up for my mistakes. But I'm no match for my mother at repartee. When it comes to verbal sparring, she's Joe Louis and Rocky Marciano and Sugar Ray Robinson all rolled into one—*and does she know it!*

"I'll make you a deal," says my mother. "You do this for me and I'll test Dr. Fradkin out for you. Rules or no rules. How's that?"

"I don't think this is a good idea," I say.

Since her divorce, my mother has grown obsessed with her own past: visiting the New Haven bus station where she first met my father, tracking down her classmates from the Hawthorne School for Girls and from Radcliff. It's as though she's researching her own obituary. Today, she wants to return to the Grand Concourse in the Bronx—to show me where her parents died.

"I *do not* understand you, Lydia." My mother lowers her voice to a whisper—but it is the peremptory, nun-like whisper that always makes me feel like a changeling. "I do not *pretend* to understand you," she says. "What sort of girl wouldn't want to know about her own grandparents?"

"Can't you just *tell* me about them?"

"That's like telling someone about heartbreak," answers my mother. "Some things you have to experience first-hand."

I concede there are some things one *does* have to experience first-hand: love, sex, pregnancy. But the deaths of my grandparents? To me, Sid and Adele Landau are black-and-white strangers lounging on the beach at Far Rockaway. He is bare-chested and paunchy; her stout face is frozen in eternal laughter. They are both voiceless, utterly without personality. *Nothing* can make them real. Yet I do want answers. I want to know what drives a healthy, vivacious woman to jump off a jetty in the middle of winter—and that means driving my mother down a lane of bad memories.

"I'll leave all my razor blades and pills at home," she offers. "Even my shoelaces, if that makes you more comfortable."

"I give up," I say. "You win."

My mother leans over and kisses me on the forehead. "Good girl," she says, as though complimenting a parrot.

I am thinking of the baby. They say a fetus can absorb knowledge in the womb, that you should play her Mozart and Haydn. Instead, my daughter will explore the South Bronx—and absorb what? The staccato of gunfire?

She'll be one tough baby. If I decide to keep her, that is.

· · · · ·

The Grand Concourse, once the Champs-Elysées of the Bronx, is now lined with Spanish-speaking travel agencies and discount tax preparers and storefront dentists advertising *no cash down*. Every block boasts a barbershop and a corner bodega. On any other street, these small businesses would suggest communal energy and a revitalizing entrepreneurial spirit—but the Concourse is too wide, too stately, maybe even too arrogant to reinvent itself as a commercial strip. Placards announcing 24-hr BBQ or promoting "ultra-sizzlin" R&B albums seem out of place beside the Art Deco facades and crenelated roofs unchanged since the days of Joe DiMaggio. The neighborhood is thriving, yet as much a ruin as Petra or Pompeii.

We park at a metered space. While I fish in my purse for quarters, my mother lights a cigarette. "That's the spot right there," she says. "In front of the firehouse."

"Okay," I say. What else is there to say? Engine Company No. 7 / Ladder Company No. 128 appears no different from any other fire station. If not for the memorial to the firefighters who died on 9-11—a bronze plaque, Polaroid snapshots, yellow ribbons—this could easily be our local firehouse in West Salem. The flag flutters at half-mast: I imagine some public servant has died in the line of duty, but not someone I know. Both sets of red garage doors are closed. There is no public symbol to mark my grandfather's place of death.

"He had a heart attack, right?" I ask.

"On the way back from the candy store," says my mother. "That was forty-one years ago, remember. They didn't move people back then. The firemen just stood around and watched."

"That's awful," I say. "I'm sorry."

I'm suddenly conscious that we're two well-dressed white women on a street where two well-dressed white women are rarely seen. Pedestrians look us over as they go by, none too friendly. An obese

Black woman pushing twins in a baby carriage pauses directly in front of us. She has ample room to pass. Instead, she waits for me to step aside—and I do. "We ain't no tourist attraction," she grumbles.

"Good old Bronx charm," says my mother. "Different color, same attitude."

"We've seen the place," I say. "Ready to go?"

A lanky, copper-skinned old man steps into our conversation. He has enormous flounder eyes and is wearing a felt hat. "Don't you be afraid, ladies," he says. "The Bronx is the safest place in New York."

I step backwards, wrapping my hands around my purse.

The man grins. "Nobody gonna fly no airplanes into the Concourse."

In spite of myself, I smile. The man introduces himself as Doctor Ed. "Like the talking horse," he says. "Only doctor."

"We were actually just leaving," I say.

"Of course, lady. But if you want, I'll be glad to show you around. Take you inside the buildings, maybe—where you once lived. Best one-man tour on skid row."

"Thank you," I say. "Maybe another time."

"Sure thing. I'll be right here. Doctor Ed—though I'm not no medical doctor."

He tips his hat at each of us.

"My father died here," says my mother. "Right where you're standing."

"I'm sorry, lady," the man answers, removing his hat.

"Let's go, Mom," I say.

"Not yet. I want to go inside."

That's when I first notice a door at the side of the firehouse. It is slightly elevated—like a casket door—with a red milk crate serving as a stair. Ailanthus trees and sumac poke though the surrounding concrete. My mother crosses the sidewalk quickly and enters the building; I have no choice but to follow.

"We shouldn't be in here," I say.

"It's a public building," says my mother. "I'm the public."

The interior of the firehouse is dim and clammy, more suited for sea lions or walruses than firemen. We encounter several desks stacked high with manila folders, but no fire poles, no Dalmatians, not even a fire extinguisher. The fireman who finally stops us has round glasses and a bristly auburn mustache—he *looks* like a walrus.

"Can I help you?" he asks.

"It's too late for that," snaps my mother. "You should have thought of that forty-one years ago."

Fireman Walrus smiles, puzzled. "What's that?"

"We didn't mean to disturb you," I apologize. "My mother's father died here. She just wanted to see the place."

The fireman's features soften. "I'm really sorry," he says. "Please take a look around." He fingers his mustache. "What years was he on the force?"

"I was unclear," I say. "He wasn't a fireman. He died outside. On the sidewalk."

"You should have helped him," says my mother. "You should have *tried*."

"Please, Mom. That was four decades ago. It's not this man's fault."

I offer the fireman my most remorseful look. He has folded his arms across his expansive chest and is no longer smiling.

"Then it's his father's fault," says my mother. "Or his uncle's. They're all related, you know."

My mother does not realize that she is embarrassing herself— embarrassing us both. But I can't say much without appearing disloyal and embarrassing us further.

"I can't let you stay here," says Fireman Walrus.

In response, my mother turns and walks out. When I catch up, I take her hand and steer her towards my car.

Doctor Ed is now sitting on a nearby stoop. "Tell me something, ladies," he calls out. "Are you two Jewish people?"

I pick up my pace. My mother stops walking.

"Yes, we are," she says. "Are you?"

"I got nothing against the Jewish peoples," says Doctor Ed. "Abe Lincoln was Jewish, you know, and he done freed my ancestors."

"I didn't know," says my mother.

"Yes, ma'am. He was shot in the temple."

This is too much. "I'm exhausted," I say. "Let's go home."

"We're only halfway done, Lydia. Don't you want to know about your grandmother?"

I'm tempted to say: *No! I don't give a damn about my grand-mother.* Which—in some respects—is true. How can I connect with the death of a woman I've never met?

"Let's walk," says my mother. "For old times sake."

I look over my shoulder. Doctor Ed is following us.

"I think you should find a fireman," my mother says to me. "Firemen make good fathers—they're good at carrying things. But not *that* one. He wasn't very friendly."

· · · · ·

My mother's old building occupies an entire city block north of 175th Street. It is named for an obscure signer of the Declaration of Independence. Across the street are a bingo parlor that was formerly an Orthodox synagogue, and a one-time movie theater whose marquee now reads: "Coming Soon: Jesus Christ." In the traffic island, an ancient, pasty woman feeds crusts to the pigeons and grackles. Long gone are the crimson sidewalk-carpet and the satin-gloved doormen.

An officer of the Housing Police guards the porte-cochère. He is reading a copy of the *New York Post*.

My mother surveys the buzzer panel. She presses the button for 11J decisively.

No answer.

She presses the button again. I feel like a push-in robber—and an incompetent one at that. A female voice answers through the intercom: "Whatever it is, I don't want it. *No me molesta!*"

This does not faze my mother. "Bronx charm," she explains.

She approaches the housing cop. "Excuse me," she says. "I used to live here."

The officer looks up indifferently. He is much younger than I am.

"Would you mind letting us in?" asks my mother.

"These are private apartments," he says. "Can't help you."

"My mother died here," continues my mother. "On the eleventh floor."

"Tenants and their guests only," he answers. He must feel this isn't enough, because he adds: "Look, those are the rules."

Without warning, I feel a hand on my back. Doctor Ed has wrapped one arm around my shoulders, the other around my mothers'. "It's okay, Carlos," he says. "They're with me. Right, ladies?"

I nod.

Our elderly guide removes a Rolodex of keys from his slacks. He tries several before one opens the interior door.

"My tours are famous," he says. "Better than Hollywood. You ladies wanna see where Uncle Miltie grew up? Where Steve Lawrence met Eydie Gorme?"

"I want to see where Mama died," says my mother.

"Sure thing," agrees our guide. "Yessiree."

While we wait for the elevator, Doctor Ed tells us that as a kid he once met Charlie Keller. I have never heard of Charlie Keller, the outfielder who replaced Babe Ruth, but our guide is enormously impressed—as though he's had an audience with the pope. It crosses my mind that our pathfinder may have been drinking.

The elevator jolts as it passes each landing. The eleventh floor stinks of stale tobacco.

Doctor Ed knocks on the door of apartment J. "Open sesame," he says.

We hear several bolts turn and a sliver of face appears at a crack in the door. A female voice demands: *"Qué quiere?"*

"I got some white folks here who used to live in your apartment," says our guide. "They'll pay you fifty bucks for a look around."

I should be angry that our guide is so fast and loose with my money—fifty dollars is an hour of yoga instruction—but I'm actually grateful he hasn't offered more. I could easily be out five hundred dollars, even five thousand.

Doctor Ed steps away from the door so the tenant can see us. I feel her eyes evaluating—as though this were a police line-up.

"My mother's been sick," I say. "She wants to see where she grew up. Just for a minute or two."

"Okay," says the woman. "But money first."

Our guide holds out his hand and I pass him five tens. He slides them through the gap in the door. A moment later, it shuts completely so the woman can undo the chain. I suspect she has also concealed the money.

"I live here only four years," says the woman. "I not know the *historia.*"

She is round-faced, large-breasted—probably my age, but not well put-together. Her upper lip could use waxing, and premature gray tufts of hair protrude above her ears. She is visibly pregnant. In the sunken living room, two pudgy toddlers are watching television cartoons. The reception is poor.

"My daughter's also pregnant," announced my mother.

The woman smiles—now we have a bond. "Do you have a date yet?" she asks.

"Not for a while," I say.

"I'm Jeca," she says. "My baby, she's gonna be Jasmín."

My mother has crossed into the adjacent dining room. "I hardly recognize anything," she says. "There used to be a mahogany table here. That's where Papa did the shock therapy."

"My grandfather was a psychiatrist," I explain. "A long time ago."

"A famous psychiatrist," adds my mother. "He was an expert on bereavement. Ironic, isn't it?"

"I think we've seen enough," I say.

"Whatever you wish, lady," says Doctor Ed. "But you might as well get your money's worth."

Maybe our hostess feels guilty about taking cash from another expecting mother, because she adds: "Would you like to see the bedrooms?"

"No," I say.

"Yes," says my mother.

Doctor Ed and I stand in the doorway while Jeca leads my mother around the larger of the bedrooms. This must be where my grandparents slept. Our hostess has redecorated in pink and grey. Dozens of baby pictures frame the bureau mirror. A stuffed elephant rests on the bedspread. I sense this plush animal belongs to Jeca, not to the boys in the living room.

My mother walks to the closet. "May I?"

Jeca nods and my mother draws open the double doors, exposing a crammed wardrobe and several rows of shoes.

"There," says my mother. "That's where she did it."

"Did what?" asks out hostess.

I don't *know* the answer—but I suddenly suspect it.

"Right from that beam," continues my mother. "With Papa's belt."

"I do not understand," says Jeca.

My mother stiffens. "All right," she says. "Enough."

She does not thank our hostess, makes no effort to explain. She merely walks out of the apartment and down the stairs to the street. I am not sure whether I want to cry or throw up. I'm not yet prepared to connect the stout, jolly woman from the Far Rockaway beach with this musty, cramped closet.

Our guide pats my arm. "It's okay," he says.

His tenderness surprises me.

"You go home," he says. "It'll make better sense there."

"Thank you," I say. "And for everything."

We wait for the elevator.

I have no small bills left in my change purse, only twenties. I probably have another ten buried among my emery boards and cold remedies, but I don't want to empty out my pocketbook in a sketchy apartment corridor. Nor do I feel right asking our guide to make change.

"Here you go," I say. "We appreciate it."

Doctor Ed frowns. "What makes you think I want your money? Just because I'm a skid row drunk doesn't mean I ask for handouts."

Then he reaches for the bill and pockets it quickly.

He flashes his teeth. "But if you insist," he says.

· · · · ·

When I reach the street, my mother starts walking. I accompany her up the boulevard—away from our car. We don't speak. Eventually, we cross Fordham Road and my mother ducks into a dingy coffee shop. The building used to house a bank. An engraving on the granite façade warns: "If you know how to spend less than you get, you have the philosopher's stone." Beneath it, another sign advertises the adjacent smut shop: "Ask about our chocolate body topping." We slide into a secluded booth across from a revolving case of colorful desserts. I know they look better than they taste.

Still, my mother says nothing. A teenage girl at the opposite table is eating alone, periodically rocking a baby in a stroller.

"Mom?" I say.

"That wasn't the right apartment." My mother's eyes are icy. "Your grandmother *did* hang herself in the bedroom closet after Papa died—but not *that* closet."

"But you said 11J . . ."

"I got confused, I guess."

"What do you mean you got confused?"

"I don't know," she says. "I knew it was wrong the moment I walked in . . ."

My mother's hands are resting on the tabletop. Her skin is blotchy, her knuckles twisted and knobby like tree knots. She dabs the corners of her eyes with a paper napkin—the first time, I realize, I've ever seen her cry.

"I just don't know, Lydia," she says. "It was the most important place in my entire life and now I can't even find it . . ."

The busboy slaps two water glasses in front of us. He pulls a pair of glossy menus from his apron. At the next table, the teenager is cradling her baby in her arms.

"Maybe I should marry a busboy," I say. "They're good at carrying things."

I intend this to be a joke—but my mother doesn't smile.

"I thought the baby would make me better," she says. "I wanted to be better for the baby . . ."

"Look, Mom," I say. "I don't know how to tell you this, but... there isn't going to be a baby."

"No baby?"

I shake my head. "No baby."

"I thought you had a check-up... tests..."

"I got confused too," I say. "I'm sorry."

And I am sorry—sorrier than she can imagine—but what choice do I have? I can't tell her that it is *her fault* that there will be no baby—that I can't care for both my mother and a new daughter at once. At least, not alone. Not yet. Maybe someone else could: someone stronger, braver—someone like my mother. But not me. I reach across the table and clasp her dry hand. "There never was a baby," I say. My words sound decisive; I have almost convinced myself.

"But there *has* to be a baby," insists my mother.

The baby at the next table begins to cry.

My mother draws back her hand. "What's the point if there's no baby?"

I do not have time to answer—if an answer exists. My mother springs suddenly from the booth and yanks the sobbing child from the startled teenagers arms. The girl cries out as though slashed with glass. My mother darts toward the door.

"*Mi bebe!*" shouts the girl. "*Ayudame! Mi bebe! My baby!*"

Without warning, she jumps on me. She is shouting and cursing in Spanish—demanding the return of her child. I feel clumps of hair being pulled from my scalp. In a surge of blind frenzy, I swing her off me.

Outside is a battle zone. Two patrol cars are already on the scene. An engine from the local firehouse pulls up just as I exit the coffee shop. Fireman Walrus is perched on one of the running boards.

My mother is kneeling beside a fire hydrant. She has lost one of her shoes. Her legs jut out at unnatural angles, leaking blood and tissue onto the concrete. Miraculously, the baby appears uninjured by her fall. The child is actually smiling. *My mother is also smiling.* Both seem utterly oblivious to the sirens, the shouting, the circle of onlookers who dare not approach.

. . . . .

I follow my mother's ambulance back to Abington Manor. The girl has agreed not to press charges—her baby is unharmed. She has limited bargaining power: I have a large, bloody gash at the base of my skull and deep scratch marks beneath my eyes. Besides, I've promised medical checkups for both her and the baby. My mother will have to help me with the finances. There is no other option.

So what now?

We are the lead story on the local radio news: "In a bizarre incident this afternoon..."

Once my mother is safely ensconced at Abington, I drive aimlessly back toward the Concourse.

The Bronx seems more itself at night. A light rain is falling and the streets are nearly deserted. It is possible to look down the boulevard and to imagine the Concourse in all of its lost glory. I can imagine my grandparents, arm in arm, wishing good evening to a white-gloved doorman and strolling up the street for a cup of coffee. But it is impossible to imagine what they are talking about, how they say it, who they were...

I pull up in front of the dingy coffee shop. It is nearly midnight. I can see through the plate glass that the dive has few customers: a couple of men in blue sanitation uniforms chatting at the counter. Even the dessert case has stopped spinning.

The sidewalk outside is now quiet. Hosed down, littered up. Nothing distinguishes this corner from any other city corner, this fire hydrant from any other fire hydrant. I stand under the pink streetlight and sob—for my mother *and* for my grandmother—in a place that already matters to nobody except for me.

Measures of Sorrow

· ·

I'd taken an apartment on the wrong side of the park. This was pre-gentrification, before community empowerment, when the neighborhood's leading commercial enterprise was No-Eyed Jack, a blind barber who cut hair for tourists. My acquaintances were quick to note other local resources: "a wide array of pawn shops"; "check cashing on every corner"; "national leadership in tire irons per capita." Their warnings didn't faze me. I was a born-and-bred New Yorker, after all, city-savvy as a street urchin, and I looked forward to the cachet that my address—on an avenue named for an obscure president and then renamed for an obscure Civil Rights leader—might carry with left-wing coeds at Greenwich Village parties. Besides, it was all I could afford.

What I call "an apartment" was, properly speaking, a semi-finished basement in a once-luxurious prewar brownstone. My door opened onto a narrow, pipe-lined corridor; the windows afforded a knee-level view of the sidewalk. Men sent to read the water meter frequently mistook me for the building superintendent. This responsibility actually fell to Hector Acosta, an adult son of the Dominican landlady, who also raised gamecocks on the rear fire escapes. Two dozen roosters crowed me awake every dawn. Otherwise, I had no complaints. My new neighbors saw me as a novelty, rather than a pioneer, so they welcomed me warmly.

Crossing the park proved another matter. That no-man's-land between police precincts offered the only practicable route to the university—no cabbie wanted a cross-park fare—but its deserted trails concealed machete-wielding opium fiends and sociopaths set to garrote me with piano wire. Or so I imagined. My parents had raised me on the hazards of urban parkland; the revival of *I'm Not Rappaport* rekindled my suspicions. Although I walked briskly—with my right fist in my jacket pocket, where a would-be attacker might mistake it for a handgun—these trips to and from campus framed my days with terror. When other students asked about safety, I feigned nonchalance. My stock reply was: *I've only been axe-murdered twice.* Why admit that in mid-September, I was already alarmed over the shortening days, panicked that my schedule might converge with the twilight? Months of intense anxiety had left me ready to embrace the most ludicrous of alternatives. Which is, more or less, what I did.

· · · · ·

It was a Saturday afternoon—one final huff of torrid Indian summer. I'd just returned from a sidewalk sale, where I'd purchased two small bookcases and a stepladder to use in changing light bulbs. The bookcases were light, but bulky. Exhausting to carry three long blocks. I ditched them in the passage, propping open the door, then retreated into the kitchenette for a root beer. Holding an icy aluminum can to my forehead was far cheaper than air-conditioning. So was soaking my t-shirt in cold tap water and drawing it over my head. When I looked up, sensing a shadow, I found myself face to face with a sharp-featured, cocoa-skinned stranger—a presence as unlikely as the Cheshire cat. The man might have been twenty-five. Or forty. He wore an aloha shirt, sunglasses tucked into the collar. His arrival dazed me so thoroughly that I forgot to shout for help.

"The day is very hot," said the intruder. "Not a day for the transporting of furniture."

Even by Manhattan standards, this development was unprecedented: a stranger had followed me into my apartment to report the weather. He'd also carried my bookshelves inside and deposited them behind the sofa.

"You are wondering from where I come," said the intruder, who *did* speak with an accent—though his origins hadn't crossed my mind. "I once told people that I come from a nation of which they have never heard," he explained. "But that is not of interest to most people. There are *many* nations of which nobody has ever heard. So now I say that I come from a nation no longer in existence, an island under lava, which is as much the truth. This is of interest to them far more."

I caught sight of a screwdriver on the countertop, and considered lunging for it, but my intruder no longer seemed threatening. Merely inept. Muggers didn't wear open-toed sandals. Nor could I imagine one so self-possessed. You'd have thought that in the man's Caribbean birthplace—which he named and which I *hadn't* ever heard of—the *custom* was to follow strangers home.

The intruder extended a hand nearly as large as a baseball glove, but a bit awkwardly, as though handshakes were not among his island's traditions. "Ollie," he introduced himself. "I am residing on the second floor."

I kept my arms at my sides. "Do you want something?"

Ollie answered with a mesmeric smile—one that announced: *If I do want something, I'll find a way to get it.* He had teeth as white as meerschaum, but jagged, and canines like alabaster stalactites.

"May I sit down?"

I said nothing. My visitor removed a cardboard box from a nearby folding chair and seated himself in reverse, his elbows resting on the squared-off back. He'd brought with him a small stack of books, which he'd placed on the carpet and which he adjusted periodically, maybe to emphasize his ownership.

"I think more clearly when I am sitting down," he said.

"I'm rather busy," I answered.

"The blood has less gravity against which to fight, sitting down."

I walked to the kitchen table—no longer feeling endangered, merely annoyed—and, in an effort to appear busy, sorted through the previous day's mail. "I have a dissertation to write," I said.

"It is for that reason I have come to see you."

Our interaction had advanced from the implausible to the impossible. My dissertation in the Department of Judaic Studies examined two ancient Hebraic commentaries on sorrow. According to Beit Hillel, the precise number of tears to be shed before the Messiah's arrival was fixed. Those not wept in one generation would inevitably pour forth in another. A second school, Beit Shammai, rejected this interpretation. These rabbis maintained it was the volume of tears, not their number, that was predetermined. No layperson in their right mind could have cared less.

"You're interested in *my* dissertation?"

"I am interested," said Ollie, "in your knowledge."

"Meaning?"

"I want you to teach me. To tutor me."

Tutor him? He was lucky I hadn't stabbed him. "In what?"

Ollie paused—either to collect his thoughts or for dramatic effect.

"Everything," he said. "Everything that they teach at the university."

I expected Ollie to grin—to reveal a joke at my expense—but he didn't. He couldn't have been more serious had he sought religious instruction from a monk. "I have been attempting on my own," he added, passing me his collection of books. "I have learned that you cannot learn everything on you own. You need a teacher to place your knowledge in order."

His three books were Heidegger's *Being and Time*, Packenham's *History of the Boer War* and *The Complete Short Novels of D. H. Lawrence, Volume II*.

"Order is important," I conceded.

"So you will teach me?"

I thumbed aimlessly through Heidegger. The dog-eared paper-back had lost its cover and the pages flaked easily. Some sentences were highlighted in red. Others in yellow. Question marks cluttered the margins. Although I hoped to avoid bad blood, particularly with a fellow tenant, I refused to yield under pressure.

"*I don't know you.*" I drifted toward the door, hoping he'd follow. "I'm sure if you phone the university, there are always graduate students looking for money . . ."

Ollie shook his head. "I do not have that amount of money," he answered. "I am driving a taxicab."

"So you want me to teach you *for free?*"

"For trade." He stood up and rested one of his feet on the chair, his elbow braced against his elevated knee. "I have seen you crossing the park," he explained. "You move like a fox in a dog pound."

I snapped shut his book. "So?"

"So I will be your chauffeur. I will drive you to the university and I will drive you from the university." Now, he grinned. "No more fox-trotting."

"In return for . . . ?"

Ollie didn't answer directly. "They say this is the land of opportunity," he said. "*You* are my opportunity."

He extended his oversized hand again. "Let us shake upon it."

"I'll think it over," I said.

"No, no. Let us shake upon it and I will drive you now."

I had no reason to visit the campus on a Saturday afternoon, nor was I clear about my attitude toward this man's odd proposition, but I am non-confrontational by nature, and a ride in his taxi seemed preferable to further argument. So I shook his hand. He held mine a bit too long, the sort of clasping, fleshy handshake that Bible-thumpers attribute to homosexuals. But there was no hint of the romantic in his smile. If anything, his expression was *too familiar* for romance. *Too confident.* I wasn't at all surprised when he stepped backwards and sized me up—the sort of "second look" one might give to auction-bought livestock. He nodded. He appeared to believe that he'd struck a winning bargain.

Outside the skies had turned dark. Thunder rumbled in the distance. We found Ollie's cab blocking a bus stop, a bright orange summons under one wiper blade.

"Do not be alarmed," said Ollie, as though a parking ticket might presage nuclear winter. He tucked the summons into his shirt pocket. "It is a trick. An empty envelope that I obtained last year from an abandoned automobile."

"Clever," I said—although this was an ancient ploy.

"Only when used properly." He removed a flyer from the windshield. It read: THIS VEHICLE HAS BEEN TOWED TO THIS LOCATION BY THE NEW YORK CITY POLICE DEPARTMENT. DO NOT SUMMONS. The date and a NYPD insignia followed. "I print these in the public library."

When I settled into the passenger seat, I spotted another of my new acquaintance's deceptions. Ollie's taxi was a large yellow Crown Victoria with a service light on the roof—but it was *not* a "yellow cab." The hood lacked the necessary medallion. In New York City, I warned him, that's a prison offense.

"Which is the *true* crime?" answered Ollie. "To drive without a medallion? Or to limit the number of taxicabs by artificial measures? They say this is the land of capitalism. I am capitalizing."

Ollie rolled down his window and lit a cigarillo. Not the moment, I decided, for a crash-course on market regulation.

"Can I ask you something?" I asked. "What's this all about? Why this urge to know *everything*? Most people hardly know anything."

"I will tell you," answered Ollie. "It is not so remarkable. I am wishing to make an impression upon a woman."

That I could relate to. I had once memorized all of Shakespeare's sonnets to win the heart of a folksinger. It didn't work—but the failure left me with a soft spot for quixotic ventures.

"Who is she?" I asked.

"She is a graduate student at your university. Her name I do not know."

I responded with matching syntax. "Her name you do not know?"

"Her name I do not know."

I waited for Ollie to say more, but he didn't. Instead, he honked his horn at pedestrians edging into a crosswalk.

"What *do* you know about her?" I asked.

"I picked her up two weeks ago. I remember the precise date. It is the same date upon which I picked her up last year."

"Let me get this straight. You want to impress a girl whose name you don't even know because you've given her two rides on the same date."

"Not at all," answered Ollie. "I am wishing to make an impression upon her because she is most beautiful woman I have ever seen. That I have picked her up two times on the same date is a sign that I may succeed. You have read the play *Romeo and Juliet*? I believe that Romeo falls in love with Juliet before learning of her name."

"Jesus Christ. You've got it all figured out, don't you?"

"I have never picked up another passenger twice. On any days." His expression turned grave, almost wistful. "A beautiful woman is not easy to obtain," he added. "One must seize one's opportunities."

Ollie tossed his cigarillo out the window and eased the cab to the curb. Broadway and 116th Street. "As you say in this country," he said. "Door to the door service."

Rain was falling in heavy, piercing drops. Ollie let me off and pulled back into traffic. I realized, too late, that I hadn't arranged for a ride home—that I had no choice but to "fox-trot" across the park.

·····

Our first "lesson" took place the following evening in Ollie's apartment. He occupied a cozy studio overlooking a neglected yard. School kids had appropriated this lot for a battlefield, raising a fort from discarded cinderblocks. There were also two abandoned bathtubs in which an elderly woman cultivated marigolds. What had once been a stockade fence lay rotting in the crabgrass. Inside, Ollie's quarters were sparsely furnished and so immaculately clean that I'd have licked sorbet off the linoleum. But the room conspicuously lacked personal landmarks. No photographs. No souvenirs. Its most distinguishing feature was a well-manicured spider plant. The sterility reminded me of the model units that resorts use to market timeshares.

Crafting a curriculum that encompassed "everything" posed a challenge, particularly because of Ollie's haphazard knowledge-base. He could name the popes dating back to Boniface VIII—and their dates of service—but he'd never heard of Annie Oakley or Charles Lindbergh. I joked that he should read all the books in the library alphabetically, like the Self-Taught Man in Sartre's *Nausea*, but he took my suggestion quite seriously, and rejected it. *If I did that*, he said, *you would be unnecessary*. So we started at the beginning: Homer. Thales. Anaximander. Initially, I had envisioned myself a present day Henry Higgins. In reality, Ollie learned far better than I taught. He read with an intensity that most college freshmen reserve for alcohol—transforming our "lessons" into fast-paced discussions that often left *me* feeling undereducated. In the course of our first week, we ploughed through Thucydides, Xenophon, Aristotle.

The enterprise proved more pleasant than I'd anticipated. Graduate students have few social outlets, and even fewer opportunities to produce anything tangible, so I took pride in Ollie's expanding knowledge, much as a stonemason might in a rising cathedral. Also, grudgingly, I grew to enjoy his company. It was impossible not to. My student's homespun theories of justice, as entertaining as they were ass-backwards, rivaled the best of Mark Twain or Shalom Aleichem.

One autumn evening, when we were about six weeks into our survey of all previous thought, a photograph appeared on Ollie's desolate bureau: a candid shot of a brunette smoking in a café. To say she was "beautiful"—you might as easily describe Mozart as "musical" or Caligula as "unpleasant." I have never seen hair so black or skin so white. The girl was laughing, eyes closed, mouth open, like the women in beer advertisements. I tried my best to ignore her, to focus on Seneca's tragedies. I was Ollie's tutor, after all, not his confidante, nor did I wish to give him the satisfaction of showing my curiosity. But even from a photograph, the girl's looks were head-turning.

"Okay, you win," I finally said. "Who's that?"

"Laurah Townsend," Ollie replied—as though the picture had been collecting dust on his dresser for decades.

I'd grown accustomed to these oblique answers, to the cat-and-mouse routine that usually followed. "Who is Laurah Townsend?"

"The woman I am wishing to marry," he said. "She spells it with an 'h.' Laurah. Do you believe one pronounces it differently?"

Somehow the stakes had risen to matrimony. "How'd you get the picture?"

"I followed her from her place of residence," he said. "I was very careful to record the address when I dropped her off."

"That's stalking," I objected. "You can't do that."

"Scouting, my friend. Not stalking. If I had been a Shakespearean hero, I would have sent forward a messenger to make inquiries."

"If you'd have been Cro-Magnon man," I snapped, "you'd have clubbed her and dragged her back to your cave. *In this country*, it's goddam stalking."

Ollie kneaded his forehead with his fingertips. Then he crossed to the window and began watering the spider plant from a green plastic pitcher.

I found myself second-guessing my outburst, wondering whether he might take it for xenophobia. Or worse.

"This is very healthy," he finally said. "As in the *Dialogues* of Plato. We are sharing a difference of opinion."

I shook my raised fist à la Jackie Gleason—but smiled in spite of myself. "Did anybody ever tell you that you're infuriating?" I asked.

"The watering of plants I find relaxing," Ollie answered, apropos of nothing. "It is like urinating on an empty bladder."

"Seneca," I prompted. *"Hercules Oetaeus."*

"You have now seen Laurah Townsend. Do you think you will able to help me to date a woman like that?"

"I don't know if *I* could date a woman like that."

Ollie looked up from the plant. "You do not have to do so," he answered. "That is not of importance."

. . . . .

While my student/chauffeur knew no shame in flouting automobile regulations—it eventually came out that he even lacked liability insurance—Ollie kept his bargain with me to the letter. (*"We* have an agreement," he explained. "With the State of New York, I do not have an agreement.") Every weekday morning, at precisely eight-thirty, Ollie's cab pulled up to our stoop. His arrivals were as punctual as Mussolini's trains, as consistent as Immanuel Kant's afternoon strolls—which, we read in November, the house-wives of Königsberg once used to set their clocks. The regularity of our departures contrasted with the timing of my return trips. These grew earlier by the day. I spent increasingly more energy brushing up my Shakespeare (and Milton and Dryden and Swift), concomitantly less quantifying unhappiness. Even in the world of Talmudic studies, my dissertation seemed iconically trivial: who cared about the relationship between liquid cubits and fluid ounces? Or precisely *how much* Rachel wept for her children? Expo-sure to the classics had torn off my blinders. I degenerated into one of those ghostly graduate students who publish nothing, yet are passionately engaged in maintaining the illusion of scholarship.

My commercial activity also shifted away from the campus. I washed my clothing at the corner laundromat that doubled as a bingo parlor. I bought groceries from a tiny Korean woman who made change through bulletproof glass. I even registered to vote at the local firehouse, although our precinct hadn't had a contested election since the days of Father Divine. In a matter of months, freed from the daily terror of crossing the park, I felt more comfortable in my new haunts than I ever had in my old ones. When the animal warden commandeered Hector's roosters—the same police force that couldn't keep crack out of our playgrounds—my indignation matched that of the most belligerent community activists. If I'd once been the only graduate student in the Department of Judaic Stud-ies who apologized for Al Sharpton, now I admired him. However, my true baptism didn't occur until after the New Year—sometime between Mill and Darwin—when I braved a trim at No-Eyed Jack's.

This tourist landmark was located on the far side of the boule-vard, sandwiched between a Western Union office and a storefront

church. It had only one barber chair. The "hot seat" faced several
rows of cushion-lined benches from which, every weekday afternoon, and all day Saturdays, tourists paid to watch the maestro at
his craft. (Jack had an arrangement with a sightseeing company
that also organized gospel brunches. They provided the audience;
he supplied the show.) The walls displayed photographs of the
barber in the company of a wide assortment of celebrities, including an enormous portrait of him with his arms draped over the
shoulders of Stevie Wonder and Ray Charles. Taped to a support
beam, between two sections of mirror, a sign announced: IF I
WERE WHITE, I'D BE A SURGEON. During performances, Jack
sported garish monochrome suits in chartreuse, mauve and ver-
million. On weekday mornings, serving a local clientele, he didn't
bother to tuck his t-shirt into his dungarees.

I settled into the barber chair and asked for a trim, hoping the
man was a fraud. My stomach quivered when he removed his
glasses to reveal two porcelain eyes.

"We was wondering when you'd come in here, Teach," he said.

I wasn't sure whether to answer. I did not want to distract him.
"You know me?"

"Everybody knows ya, Teach. You're the guy is teaching Ollie."

Where was this leading? I wondered. Would I end up instructing
the barber's children in Sanskrit?

"Ollie comes in here?" I asked.

"Everybody come in here," said the barber.

He ran his calloused fingers over my scalp, my brow, my neck.
I'd heard he shaved men with a straight razor, but I wasn't *that*
daring.

"My boy Ollie swears up down and sideways you the most excel-
lent thing since Lena Horne. Says ya gonna be best man at his
wedding."

"He said that?"

"Uh-huh. Now lean forward." Jack adjusted my head and low-ered his open scissors in front of my eyes. Then he drew back swiftly. "Before we start," he said, "you wanna see my collection of ears?"

I told myself I'd survive, because others had survived—no differ-ent than air travel or tattooing. My fingernails dug into the leather armrests.

"Don't let me be scaring ya, Teach. You can always trust a blind barber. He's got a lot more at stake."

He snipped the line of hair across my forehead. Straight as a railroad tie.

"Nobody will give you a difficult time in this neighborhood," Jack said—switching abruptly from Newyorkese to the King's Eng-lish. "You tell them where you live. They will assume that you're much worse off than they are."

. . . . .

Several months later, Ollie announced that he was "ready to practice." We were relaxing in my apartment—his ceiling had started to leak—after a lengthy discussion of the Boxer Rebellion. (I couldn't imagine Laurah Townsend bringing up John Hay's Open Door Policy on a first date, but as Ollie insisted, *everything* was *everything*.) "You will be Laurah," he explained. "I will be me." He lit a votive candle in a teacup and set it on the Formica tabletop, apparently to create ambiance.

"How can I be Laurah?" I asked. "I don't know the first thing about her."

"That does not matter. I do not either."

"So you want me to pretend to be a girl I've never met and to act as if we're out on a first date."

"Precisely," said Ollie.

"What sort of restaurant is it? What am I wearing?"

These questions were intended facetiously, aimed at exposing the absurdity of such role-playing, but instead they egged Ollie on. He drew me a floor plan of the Italian bistro and described everything from the frescos of Florentine street-life to the specials listed on the chalkboard. When he informed me I was wearing a leopard-print skirt, form-fitting and three inches above the knee, I gave in. "Okay, Okay. I get it," I said. "Whenever you're ready ..."

Ollie straightened his back, folded his hands. "Laurah," he asked—as though conducting a job interview, "in what course of study are you at the university?"

"I'm a graduate student in the Department of Judaic Studies."

"Intriguing," answered Ollie. "I too am interested in the study of Judaism."

"Are you now?"

He ignored me. "In which area of Judaism are you studying? Possibly the Mishnah? Or the Gemara? Or Prime Minister Eshkol and the Six-Day War?"

"I'm studying tears. It's not very interesting."

"I am certain it is much more interesting than you believe."

"No," I snapped. "It's not."

Ollie paused and tapped his fingertips together. "If it is not interesting, why have you chosen it as your course of study?"

I pounded my fist on the table. "Jesus-fucking-Christ. You're on a date, not running the McCarthy hearings. Don't ask questions with difficult answers."

Ollie frowned. "I did not understand that inquiry to demand a difficult answer."

"Well it did," I said.

"How so?"

I exhaled deeply and thought backwards from ten. "Try to make her feel comfortable," I advised. "Ask open-ended questions. Let the girl steer the conversation."

"Let the girl steer the conversation," echoed Ollie—surprised, as though I'd pitched Styrofoam as snack-food. "Very well. Why do *you* not ask *me* some questions? I will practice through observational learning."

"Okay," I agreed. "*That* I can manage."

But formulating questions turned out to be far more taxing than I'd anticipated. I hadn't been dating much myself that winter—okay, not at all—and my skills were somewhat rusty. I could think only of questions which called for factual answers: who invented the combustion engine? Where did Stanley find Livingstone? If the goal had been to stump Laurah, rather than to woo her, I'd have hit pay-dirt.

"Tell me about your family," I finally said. "Do you have brothers or sisters?"

This was the first I'd ever asked Ollie of his past, sensing it was a subject he preferred to avoid, but I wasn't taking advantage of our role-playing. It was the only question I could think of not suited for a game show.

Ollie's smile never wavered, but the muscles stiffened in his shoulders. "I have no brothers and no sisters," he said.

"And your parents?"

"It is important to be always forward looking," answered Ollie. "That is why I have come to America. A past is not necessary in this country. You can reinvent yourself like Mr. Gatsby."

"But Gatsby failed."

"That is not here, nor is it there. What is important is to look always toward the future. I am also thinking of the Biblical story of Lot. Does not the wife of Lot look backward? And for this transgression is she not turned to salt?"

I cupped my fist in my palm. "Maybe you do need Henry Higgins."

"Excuse me?"

"You can't use the word transgression on a date. You sound like Reinhold Niebuhr. What kind of cockeyed school did you go to anyway?"

"I did not go to school at all," answered Ollie. "I am an autodidact. Like President Lincoln. I taught myself English from a foreign service manual."

What awed me most about Ollie's admission was that, *to him*, this method of education didn't seem the slightest bit limiting. Far from it. I imagine he believed it preferable to learn the language from a government drill-book.

"Other than my use of the word transgression," asked Ollie. " How did I fare?"

"You don't want to know."

"But I do," he said. "And I have one more question. What is this you mean by these McCarthy hearings?"

$$\cdots\cdots$$

That's when my real teaching started. Ollie's greatest hurdle wasn't a shortage of information, but too much of it. Or maybe it's more accurate to say that he lacked a framework with which to distinguish common knowledge from the $64,000 question. All facts had equal value, to his thinking, until proven otherwise. He did not understand, for instance, that if you quoted Churchill, you were most likely referring to the British prime minister. You might as easily be referring to Arabella Churchill, the mistress of James II, or Canadian actor Berton Churchill. Nor was Ollie bashful about asking: *Do you mean the Augustan courtesan? Or the colleague of John Wayne? Or might you be referencing the eighteenth century general?* With some effort, I trained him to assume Winston without inquiry—a principle that he learned to generalize. Darwin was Charles, not Erasmus. Marx, unmodified, meant Karl—never Groucho. So far, so good. But why didn't the Marx Brothers include Karl, Eduard, and Hermann? And was it permissible to ask whether Chamberlain was Neville or Wilt?

All summer I taught Ollie to forget things. "Neville, okay," I said. "Maybe Wilt. But *never* Owen. As far as you're concerned, there is no Owen Chamberlain."

"Are you certain?" asked Ollie. "He was a winner of the Nobel Prize. To him we owe our entire understanding of anti-protons."

"I'm sure we do," I said. "And for that I'm truly grateful. But he is not important."

Ollie massaged the bridge of his nose. "If you say he is not of importance," he agreed without conviction, "then I will speak no more of him."

Later, of course, he would second-guess my judgment and deliver an impassioned defense of Owen Chamberlain's research on fundamental particles. *How could I not think proton-proton scattering important?* Ollie valued knowledge too much to yield it without a struggle. My task was like spring cleaning with a packrat.

And then—one morning in September—Ollie fired me. He expressed his intentions as we passed behind the cathedral, under the shedding maples, where two priests had recently been stabbed. They'd had no chauffeur. No "door to the door" service. Police barricades still cordoned off the sidewalk.

"This evening," Ollie announced, "I will dine with Laurah Townsend."

"Tonight?"

"One full year has past since she last rode in my taxicab. Two full years have passed since she first rode in my taxicab."

"But you can't. Not yet." My initial objection had been on Ollie's account—to prevent him from acting prematurely. Hadn't Branch

Rickey held back Jackie Robison? Then I realized that I stood to lose more than he did: my employer, my chauffeur, my closest friend. Ollie had placed all of his eggs in Laurah's basket. Most of mine had ended up in his. "Trust me," I said. "Let's give it another few months."

"This evening," answered Ollie. "I have already made arrangements. I picked up Laurah Townsend yesterday afternoon and invited her to dine."

"And she said yes?"

"She did not say 'no,'" said Ollie. "She laughed. This evening I will pay a visit to her café."

"Uninvited?"

"Not invited," answered Ollie. "Not *uninvited* either."

I sensed the futility of objecting further; it would have been easier to postpone a solar eclipse. Moreover, I'd lost track of my loyalties. Didn't Ollie's success mean an end to our lessons? And what would his failure mean? My next thought highlighted the absurdity of my predicament. I'd wanted to ask: *Can I come along?* Or, in the least, *Can I watch?*

"Maybe I'll drop by that café," I said. "To check up on you."

Meaning what? To play duenna? To play voyeur?

Ollie nodded thoughtfully. "I would like that very much," he said. "Like the tourists at the shop of the barber. You will be my audience."

· · · · ·

The café, Just Desserts, was located on the "right" side of the park. It had replaced Lenin's & Trotsky's, a smoke-hazy Kerouac hangout, but had retained the former establishment's Soviet décor. Warsaw Pact flags hung from the exposed rafters. Behind the cheese-cake display, placards advocated for Sacco and Vanzetti. In the men's room, a flint-faced Stalin glowered over the urinals. But the clientele had evolved: where denim-clad anarchists had once played darts, junior faculty now rehearsed lectures. Prices had also doubled. On weekends, stroller-fettered couples bought six-dollar lattes for takeout. The old and new patrons shared one characteristic: They were almost uniformly white. Not a stamping ground for Caribbean cabbies.

I arrived two hours early, hoping to snag a good seat. Laurah Townsend, as I'd anticipated, had already claimed a chair by the window. The woman was as stunning as she'd appeared in the photograph, but considerably older. Maybe thirty. Even thirty-five. She wore an angora sweater and a gray linen skirt—a far cry from the low-cut blouse and skintight pants that I'd imagined. She was writing in pencil, gnawing the stub of her eraser. Crumpled balls of yellow paper littered her workspace, and every few minutes, she increased the chaos with a page torn from a legal pad. The table's perimeter was hemmed with books. I installed myself nearby and pretended to read the newspaper. I was doing nothing wrong, I assured myself. Nothing illegal. I was no different from any other graduate student enjoying an espresso in a public coffee shop.

But I knew otherwise. I was, in Ollie's language, scouting. At one point, I peered over the newspaper and our eyes met. Laurah smiled: a tender, teasing smile that lingered until I looked away. Scouting might be sketchy; but flirting crossed the line—the sort of transgression that bordered on evil. Fortunately, the rightful suitor showed up before I had a chance to do damage.

I hardly recognized Ollie. My student had shaved his beard, traded in his sandals and beach attire for khakis and a stylish pink shirt. He winked at me, but crossed directly to Laurah—either overenthusiastic or afraid of losing his nerve. When he spoke— deliberatively, as though measuring each word—his voice held the same confidence it had that first afternoon in my apartment.

"Excuse me," said Ollie. "I believe that yesterday I had the privilege of driving you in my taxicab."

"Oh, you," said Laurah. Her surprise reminded me of my own shock at Ollie's first appearance. She flipped over her pad.

"I know what you are thinking," continued Ollie. "You are thinking that many taxicab drivers do not dine in this café."

"No," said Laurah. "I guess not."

"I drive a taxicab only to earn my livelihood. To give me leisure time to focus on my studies." Ollie leaned forward to see the titles of her books. "*Secrets of the Atom*," he read. "*Oppenheimer vs. HUAC.* You are studying physics?"

"The history of physics," said Laurah. "You've heard of Schrodinger."

"I assume that you mean Erwin Schrodinger who won the Nobel Prize for his work in quantum mechanics. It is not likely that you mean W. A. Schrodinger, the Bavarian horticulturist."

Laurah tucked her pad into her backpack—as though preparing to leave. Ollie frowned and then his expression turned unexpectedly gleeful. "Are you, by any chance, familiar with the research of Owen Chamberlain?"

"You know about Owen Chamberlain?" I could sense the girl's discomfort ebbing slightly, her appetite genuinely whetted. "*You're studying physics?*"

"Not at all," answered Ollie. "My interest is entirely avocational. I believe the research of Chamberlain is underappreciated." I did not see the man move—but somehow he ended up seated. "What I am studying," he said, "are Talmudic commentaries on tears. My hope is to quantify the sorrow in the universe."

"Tears?" asked Laurah.

"Tears."

Ollie served up a cogent, lucid summary of my thesis. He reduced seven years of research into a series of provocative anecdotes, exploring a broad swath of emotion from the humorous to the heartrending. In his voice, the project actually sounded interesting, a topic worthy of investigation. What stung me most was his self-assurance—that he never once looked in my direction.

"I am deeply interested in misfortune," Ollie concluded. "That is what happens when one is of a nation which is no longer in existence."

"Your family . . . ?" asked Laurah.

"All of them. All of my brothers and sisters," he said. And then he spoke of the cascading lava, of the horrors he had never shared with me, until the girl was dabbing away tears of her own. When I left the café, they were still locked in conversation.

The sun had already set. I drifted toward the park—bracing myself for the passage through the darkness. I carried inside me this story, of Ollie's education, and my own, but I knew nobody with whom to share it. You can measure a man's sorrow, and the world's, in the number of stories that perish unheard.

Shell Game with Organs
· ·

Houdini urges me to disappear again. That's his panacea, his sov-
ereign remedy. If he had his way, I'd vanish into thin air one night
without a trace. On Lois, on mother, on him. And I suppose that
would suit the old fellow just fine, too. The building crew would
sniff him out eventually—find him belly-up on the carpet, caked in
is own excrement, his kingdom lost for want of a saltine. Even then
he'd be croaking *Disappear* through parched lips, I imagine, ped-
dling spontaneous combustion to the Puerto Rican doorman and
the one-armed super. Houdini squeezes shut his onyx eyes, raises
his wings to his cheeks. His voice is urgent. "Disappear! Disappear!"
  "Shut up!"
  Three hours straight I've debated alternatives, judged and un-
judged myself. I don't *have* to visit mother. I don't *have* to play
the shell game with organs. After tonight's show I could stow my
equipment in the back of the truck and relocate to New York. Or
rural Mauritania. A magician pulling off a disappearing act. Nothing could be more natural.
  "How would you feel about rural Mauritania?" I ask Houdini.
"The Sahara? The Casbah?"
  Already I despise myself for shouting at him and I feed him a
chocolate-coated wafer. He clasps the treat in his beak, slides it

down his gullet with a tilt of his head. At least I can please someone, I think. So what if the snacks cause parrot cancer.

"What do you say we ditch mother and Lois and head off to Africa—just the two of us?"

"Disappear," Houdini retorts ambiguously, "Disappear." His vocabulary—the product of a magic routine we once did together—is frozen in time like a dead language.

Lois interrupts our conversation, struts in through the open door. Her heels pummel the hardwood in the foyer. We've been dating for almost a month now—which at forty-one means we're serious, that we know each other well—and still her vigor astounds me afresh at every meeting. She's so put-together, so fast-paced. She bounces through life like a wired kangaroo. If you saw her behind the counter at the crafts shop, you'd think she had kidneys.

"Ready to roll?" asks Lois. She plucks the lit cigarette from my mouth, tamps it out in the ceramic ashtray. The ashtray was stolen on a dare, appropriated from a chic downtown restaurant. I slid it into my sleeve on our first date.

"I was smoking that," I say. "Stocking up on nicotine for the hospital."

"Have a wafer," suggests Lois, popping the parrot treats like pills. "You shouldn't go to a hospital smelling like smoke."

I shouldn't go to a hospital at all, I want to answer. I shouldn't have to listen to a grown woman bleat senseless strings of gibberish.

"Mother smoked," I argue indifferently. "She won't care."

"And look what happened to her," says Lois. "Now let's get a move on. I hate being late."

"Disappear!" chimes in Houdini. "Disappear!"

I toss him another wafer, then cover his cage with an aquamarine bath towel.

· · · · ·

We don't discuss the organ shell game on the way to Mass General. It's like a marriage proposal; it demands a yes or a no. Yet with every glance at Lois—with each glimpse of her bare thighs splayed on the passenger seat—I can't help reliving last night's afterglow, can't suppress the feel of her soft hands curling my pubic hair and playing across my flanks.

"Your kidneys," she cooed, sliding her fingers between the bed sheets and the small of my back. "I can feel them."

"Do they feel good?" I instantly second-guessed my own question: The same guilt I once felt when I waved to the one-armed super.

"I wish I could borrow one," said Lois.

"I wish you could too."

The words reached my brain seconds after they left my lips. Before I could decide whether I meant them—abstractly, of course—Lois bombarded me with this "emotional donor" business. She revealed that, thanks to the wonders of modern medicine, anyone who shares a blood type can share a kidney: emotion is now thicker than blood.

"Body magic," she called it. "A shell game with organs." Three nights in the hospital and I'd have her off dialysis for life. Not to mention which, she added, the second kidney wasn't doing me any good where it was.

Lois made it sound as though she'd be doing me a favor: Relieving weight from my abdomen, giving my liver room to grow. She could have been a "Let's Make a Deal" contestant selecting Kidney #2. No emotional blackmail, no hang-dog looks. And that's probably why I like her. She's the only woman I've ever met who could compare invasive surgery to a sleight-of-hand.

"You ready for the show tonight?"

"Mother still wants me to kill her."

We're plodding through Mass Pike traffic, inching between Saturday afternoon's city-bound tide. Through the rear-view mirror I can spy into other vehicles: here's an elderly couple bickering under matching sun-visors, there's three generations of a dark-skinned family sandwiched together like cold cuts. How easy their lives look through shatterproof glass. I have seen them from the stage, admired their simple wonder. Yet tonight I fear I will view them only as kidney packaging and potential matricides.

"Did you hear me?" I ask Lois. "She keeps making that sign with her hands. Like she's trying to silence a stranger or slaughter a chicken."

"You don't know what she means by it," says Lois.

"She's my mother," I say irritably. "I can tell. How am I supposed to concentrate tonight with all this to think about—with mother slicing her throat with her finger?"

Lois doesn't add, "And with your girlfriend begging for an organ handout." Most women would do that. At least most of the women I've dated. Instead, Lois says, "That's your problem. You're the magician."

So we drive in silence, sensing that last night has changed us: she has broached the kidney question and now it hangs over our relationship like some kind of love test.

I feel the need to argue my case again: that the magician's life does not easily permit this sort of commitment. Implicit for me, if not for her, is that the kidney and commitment questions are bound together like the sleeves of a straight jacket. I have loved other women. At seventeen I would have traded a lung for a blow job, but at forty-one a kidney for love seems like a risky venture. After all, I have only one spare kidney to give.

"I want you to speak with Dr. Sandkirk," says Lois. We're in the pay parking garage at the hospital; each minute of protest will add to the meter.

"Dr. Sandkirk," is all I answer.

"Yes, Dr. Sandkirk. The nephrologist."

Then we part ways, the echo of Lois's steps reverberating against the concrete. Her dialysis treatments permit me four hours alone with my mother.

· · · · ·

Mother greets me from bed with a salvo of, "Late trees under water and each one has *his* own." That's the retired English teacher poking through, her speech without content yet impeccably grammatical. It's hard to imagine that a month ago, before the stroke, she was organizing Grey Panthers for a library boycott.

"Hi, Mom," I say, dropping a dry kiss on her leather cheek. "Bet you didn't think I was coming. "

"Late, late trees under water and each one has *his* own," she retorts. Her voice is weary, reproving. Her face looks fractured down the center and glued back together like a broken vase. When she speaks, the words bend around the corner of her mouth. She frowns at me and adds, emphatically, "Or *her* own."

I intend to tell her about the victory in the library strike, about the thousands of large print books that Boston Public has purchased under pressure. Instead, I find myself ready to shake her like an appliance on the blink. What right does she have to speak gibberish, to abandon me just when I've returned home for good? All those years on the road turning face cards into flowers, all those late night phone calls from Peoria and Yazoo City—and when I finally have a Boston gig, a sold-out debut in less than eight hours, the one person I thought I could depend on mutters, "Pills stock knowing that nurse, yes, yes," as though it were a schoolgirl's secret in need of release.

"Lois wants my kidneys," I finally say. "Well not both of them," I explain. "Only one."

In response, my mother slides her index finger across her jugular vein and closes her eyes. Her tongue falls from her mouth, her head sinks into the hospital pillows. There is no mistaking her meaning.

"I can't do that, Mother," I answer as I take her small hand in my large one. "Do you understand me? You know I can't do that. I can't. Besides, you'll be out on the picket lines in no time."

Mother opens her eyes, examines me with the wonder of a child. The doctors say the words go in with as little sense as they come out. My mother will never picket the library again, much less read a book. She is seventy-six years old. If we are lucky, chirps the underage rehabilitation therapist, she'll be able to count to ten and recite the days of the week within a year.

"Lois wants one of my kidneys," I say again. I produce a photograph from my wallet, point at Lois and then at my stomach. "Do you understand, Mother? Kid-ney." To emphasize my claim, I draw a lima bean in the air with my finger.

My mother examines the photograph carefully and frowns in confusion. She stuffs imaginary food into her mouth, shrugs her shoulders to convey a question, and then rocks a make-believe child in her arms. This is a rare breakthrough: I understand her. She wants to know whether Lois is obese or pregnant.

"Dammit, Mom," I say, "Don't do this."

I might as well threaten to punish her: "Do as you're told or your father will take off his belt." It is no use. I know the whole goddamn situation is untenable. Cruel, even. She has lost her vocabulary, her memories. And she has lived too hard, too earnestly, to squander her final years distinguishing Mondays from Wednesdays.

"I have to go now, Mom. I have a show tonight. My Boston debut. I'm going to escape from chains and a straight jacket in an underwater tank."

"Either nurse or trees," she retorts vehemently. "Neither nurse nor trees."

Somehow this means that she's angry I will not kill her. Angry she doesn't have the strength, the means, to do it herself.

My cheek is wet when I press it against hers. Then I draw back her hair, brush the purple-gray strands into place, plant my lips on her forehead.

"Hang in there," I say. "Hang in there, Mom."

My mother leans forward in her bed, reaches out toward me with ghost-walk arms. I retreat rapidly to the lobby, to the small alcove of vending machines and pay telephones. The wall clock reminds me that I still have three hours to kill, so I collapse into a vinyl chair, my mind blank, and absorb the soothing murmur of the electronic ice maker.

· · · · ·

"Rip Van Winkle returns," says Lois, startling me from my slumber. "Your twenty years are up, Rip. Time to find out who's dead and who's alive."

"Five more minutes," I say, twisting onto my side. I can feel the wooden arms of the chair jabbing my side.

"I'm going to have to get the cold water," Lois threatens. "Dr. Sandkirk doesn't have all day."

I vaguely recall this name, Sandkirk, so I blink the world into focus and rub the purple snow from my eyes. I find myself looking up into the bland, rosy face of the middle-aged physician.

Sandkirk defies my expectations. He has small round eyes, matching small round glasses. His head slopes from a broad brow to a narrow, almost inverted chin. All in all, he resembles a giant radish. So this is the celebrated nephrologist! I'd anticipated a full, glowing figure in a giant kidney costume, a man not unlike the human peach in the Fruit of the Loom underwear commercials.

"Dr. Sandkirk," Lois introduces us. "My boyfriend, Bill Sternberg, a.k.a. The Sleepy Santini."

I grumble, "The Splendid Santini," as I shake his hand.

We follow Sandkirk along a maze of corridors, pass through a series of fire proof doors. The doctor appears to know everybody. He bestows his papal wave on emaciated old women stranded in forgotten lounges and legless veterans who wheel together in packs. All the while he shares his wisdom on the topics of the day: the college selection process, the Red Sox's prospects for the pennant. When we arrive at his office, we've somehow jumped from the twelfth story to the fourteenth without switching floors. Medical magic. As yet, no mention of kidneys.

Sandkirk steers me to another vinyl chair. The office smells mildly of mildew and damp paper. The nephrologist smells pungently of aftershave lotion or raw bananas. His wall biography tells me everything I need to know. He's a Princeton graduate, a champion Little League coach, a Fellow of the American College of Physicians. All of this indicates a man with connections: one whose absence would be noted if I made him disappear.

Sandkirk says, "So, you're thinking about donating a kidney."

I answer, "That sounds like the title of a self-help book."

The doctor smiles; Lois crosses her legs.

"Thinking about it," I say. "Only thinking."

"That's good, Mr. Sternberg. I'd be the first to warn you against a hasty decision. Because there *are* risks, you understand. Of course, they're relatively minor risks. Yet they are risks. Like driving a car or flying in an airplane. You don't think about the risk every time you drive to work, but it exists nonetheless. Am I making myself clear?"

"Risks are bad," I say. That's one of the few things I know for certain.

"And yet sometimes risks are necessary," says Sandkirk. I fear he will launch into a sermon on Alexander Fleming and the history of modern medicine. Instead, he outlines the advantages and drawbacks of the emotional donor. Lois listens attentively, glances at me periodically through the corners of her eyes. Sandirk narrates my recovery from post-op stitching to outpatient check-ups. After fifteen minutes, he has me feeling as though the entire procedure is as easy as a card trick. Nothing more than a shell game with organs. It's the non-givers, Sandkirk's "reluctant potentials," whose ignorance gives transplant a bad name. I feel guilty. As though I haven't signed the cornea release on the back of my driver's license.

"Of course I'll need some blood," the nephrologist concludes. "We need to confirm blood types and check for antibodies. Lois says you're both O-positives. Now roll up your sleeve."

He's rummaging through his filing cabinet for a needle when I stand up to excuse myself. "I'll think about it, Sandkirk," I offer. "But no blood. Not now. I have a show tonight."

"He does, doctor," Lois repeats apologetically.

"Oh," says Sandkirk. "Well good luck then. I'll see you soon."

We retreat into the corridor.

"What was that about?" I demand as soon as we've escaped.

"What do you mean?"

"I mean that guy's knife-happy. I'm lucky he didn't do it right there on his desk with a scissors."

Lois laughs. A short, sharp laugh. She asks, "So is that your answer?"

"I'm thinking," I say. "Still thinking."

"Well don't think too hard," she answers—and it's impossible to tell whether she's joking or sincere. "You might rupture your brain."

Then she kisses me on the lips, feels my crotch through my jeans. A nurse passes and throws me a *This is a hospital* look over a stack of hand-crocheted sweaters.

I kiss Lois harder and disappear into the warmth of her body. I suppress the urge to shout at the departed nurse, to tell her what she can do with her hospital. So what if it's a hospital! It's not a morgue. I'm ready to give the legless vets a thrill.

Lois pushes me back. "Down Big Boy," she says. "Time to go home."

I lean in for another kiss.

"Home," she says. "Later. You have a show tonight. Remember?"

"What show?"

"Magic," she answers.

· · · · ·

I'm tired of doctors, tired of hospitals. I find myself wishing that mother would die and give Lois the kidney—and then I despise myself for the thought. That's not a solution. Not a realistic solution, at least. Vanishing, on the other hand, has a lot to be said for it. Almost too much to be said for it. Who'd miss me? I don't coach little league; I didn't go to Princeton. My alma mater, the exalted Garfield School of the Arts, went bust in the early 80's. The only two people who'd notice, who'd really notice, are Lois and mother—and with mother I don't know for certain. So there's only Lois. Lois. And, of course, Houdini. But Houdini's actively urging me to disappear.

"Disappear!" I call into the empty apartment. I pause at the kitchen table to sort through the afternoon's mail. "Isn't that right, Houdini? Disappear!"